Bloody Twine #4

Twisted Tales with Twisted Endings

Matthew L. Marlott

Bloody Twine #4

Cover art and interior art modified from public resources courtesy of Canva.com. The ad for the Bloody Twine Series at the back of this book was partially created by artificial intelligence courtesy of Canva.com.

ISBN: 978-1-964407-03-6

This book is for all who just wish to sit back, relax, and enjoy some twisted tales with twisted endings. This book is dedicated to fans of traditional horror.
If you like this book, give it a good review and tell me what your favorite story was in this collection.

Table of Contents

Preface

These stories were originally published on my own personal site, bloodytwine.com. It's a little site that has received an equal amount of little attention, but it's mine, and I'm proud of it. I use this site to perfect my stories, and thanks to it, you have these bundles of fine short horror tales you can now peruse and enjoy at your leisure.

Imagine walking into an abandoned storage room filled with old newspapers and magazines, all articles stacked in bundles neatly tied with twine, but then you discover other bundles, bundles not so neatly tied, ragged bundles of yellowed and partially-charred paper tied in bloodstained twine.

You see, some stories are meant to educate, and some stories are meant to entertain, but some stories…some stories are simply looking for a victim.

Enjoy.

Bloody Twine #4

Ah, the old "spend-the-night-in-a-haunted-house" cliché.

Vanessa stared into the darkness from within the safe confines of Ethan's truck. The house in the distance was a looming nightmare, a crowning achievement to whatever dark horror gods had actually crafted it from wood and mortar...

Average Read Time: 53m 3s

Out of the frying pan and into the fire.

This was Aaron Cordon's facility, so it was a mix of expense combined with practicality. The billionaire made sure they had what they needed, but without any extras. Shane likened the man's character to a spoiled twelve-year-old with way too much money, but that was the personality of billionaires; they didn't live in the real world...Not that it mattered much. Shane would never get to meet the man...

Average Read Time: 36m 48s

Time for horror in 2nd Person POV!

Your great-great-grandmother only lived to be sixty-three. On her deathbed, she told your great grandmother that she had been cursed by an old woman from the old country, cursed during a "picture show" back when silent films were black and white. This was back during a time when there was a cinema announcer reading off of cards, back when someone played the piano in the background during the film...

Average Read Time: 15m 15s

The title is not metaphorical.

He could see it now, and it was big. It was at least eight-feet-tall, a couple feet shorter than him, and it was slenderer than

#1...KNUCKLEBONES

Ah, the old "spend-the-night-in-a-haunted-house" cliché.

Vanessa stared into the darkness from within the safe confines of Ethan's truck. The house in the distance was a looming nightmare, a crowning achievement to whatever dark horror gods had actually crafted it from wood and mortar.

"This isn't a good idea, Ethan," she breathed out. "I don't like this one bit. We don't even have our phones..."

"I told you..." said her boyfriend. "They can track us that way."

"Who?" asked Vanessa. "Who can track us?"

"The police," shrugged Ethan. "The F.B.I....Homeland Security for all I know. Anybody that wants us to get caught. This is breaking and entering."

"We're not stealing anything," frowned Vanessa. "We're just staying the night."

"Doesn't matter to the law," replied Ethan. "They've criminalized everything anymore. You can get arrested for anything, and once you're in the system, you're screwed. I'm not risking it."

Lights shone from behind them as another truck pulled up onto this out-of-the-way dirt road that led to this haunted piece of land. They were deep in the woods, way outside of town, and no one ever came here, not ever.

"They're here," said Ethan. "Carlos and Riley. They had to make a detour to pick up Lucas."

Vanessa still didn't like this. She did not like the idea of breaking the law, but one look at the weathered and broken-down two-story house in front of them, however, was a stronger reason for not spending the night, much stronger.

"This is like the beginning of every horror movie ever," said Vanessa. "Are you sure nobody lives here?"

"In this dump?" asked Ethan. "You've got to be kidding me. This house has been abandoned for thirty years. There's nobody here…Now quit whining, and let's go be legends."

He opened the driver's-side door and exited the truck, so Vanessa had no choice but to follow.

She followed Ethan into Carlos's truck lights as Carlos, Lucas, and Riley all exited Carlos's vehicle.

The boys were all wearing their red letterman jackets with the gold lettering, but Riley had her hair dyed jet-black, and she was in her black miniskirt, black fishnet stockings, black booties, black T-shirt, and matching black leather jacket, something Vanessa would not wear in this chilly neck of the woods, or at any time, for that matter. The girl looked like a streetwalker.

Vanessa, herself, had on a simple pink jacket to match her tight pink pants, pink shirt, and vanilla-cream shoes. She liked the cuter colors, even if Riley did not.

Ethan and Carlos slapped hands together while Lucas took a long gulp from the beer in his left hand.

"Class of 2022, baby!" cried Carlos, a giant grin on his face. "We are gonna be legends!"

"Whooooo!" yelled Lucas as he crushed the empty beer can in his left hand and tossed the aluminum container off into the nearby brush.

Riley walked past Vanessa, a strange grin on her face, a fascination in her dark eyes that was visible even in the poor lighting of the two trucks parked near her. The young woman stared at the house in the distance, turned, and then shone Vanessa that weird grin, something Vanessa did not really wish to see…It was disturbing.

Vanessa was not really friends with Riley…She was not into that horror/Goth crowd or whatever it was that Riley liked. Riley was Carlos's girlfriend, though Vanessa suspected the only thing a football jock had in common with a Goth girl was the sex. Those two were well known for doing the deed in public places; they'd just never been caught by the police.

"The Faerber House," smiled Riley. "Isn't it beautiful?"

At this distance, Vanessa could see the heavy coating of black eyeshadow and black lipstick on the weird Goth girl.

Riley was kind of repulsive when Vanessa gave a second thought about it. Watching her was like watching a cockroach crawl across a kitchen countertop.

"It's gross," frowned Vanessa. "It's old and rundown and falling apart."

"I know," grinned Riley with wide eyes. "It's awesome."

"So what is this place?" asked Lucas.

Lucas was tall, blonde, and pretty hot, but everyone at school knew he only dated college girls. He used a fake ID to pretend to be a college student as he prowled the bars for one-night stands…It was common knowledge.

He walked up behind Riley and put his right arm around her shoulders.

Carlos immediately removed that right arm and pushed Lucas away, a grin on Carlos's face to match his girlfriend's.

"It's the Faerber House, numnuts," replied Carlos. "Just like she said."

"So?" asked Lucas. "What's that supposed to mean?"

"It means nobody's been here since the family that lived here disappeared thirty years ago," said Ethan. "They just up and left all their stuff and disappeared. Mom, dad, little girl…No trace of 'em."

Vanessa's boyfriend walked up and wrapped his arm around her waist. She loved him, but he was obsessed with this stupid house, and that was not a good thing. Obsessions like these always ended badly, especially when the house in question looked like it had been birthed straight out of a child's nightmare.

Nevertheless, they were here now, here at this "Faerber House," so it was time to concentrate on that. There was always some kind of ghost story, murder story, or other kind of horror story that went with these places, and she wanted to hear it.

She didn't get to ask the next question about it, though. Lucas beat her to that through sheer, straight-up denial.

"Nobody's lived here for thirty years?" snorted Lucas. "That's B.S. This place would have been sold by now."

"Nope," said Carlos. "The mom's dad still owns the place and refuses to sell it. He's in his eighties now, so this place will be up for grabs once he croaks. The old fart has no other living relatives. Owns the land around here, too."

"And no one else has come out here?" asked Lucas. "I know when I'm standing in—"

"The disappearances," interrupted Riley.

She still had that crazy grin on her face…Vanessa couldn't stand it.

"What?" asked Lucas.

"The disappearances around town," said Riley. "Over the last thirty years, fifteen people have gone missing. Four homeless people, six bikers, three travelers from out of town, one Jehovah's Witness, and one census taker."

"And?" asked Lucas.

"They all came to this house and camped out in it, genius," said Ethan. "Everybody knows that."

"B.S.," said Lucas with a roll of his eyes.

"Nobody's ever proven it, but we all know it," said Carlos.

"That is why *we* are going to be the first to spend the night here and live to tell the tale," said Ethan. "We are going to be *legends*."

"How?" asked Lucas. "You told us to leave our phones at home. We've got no way of taking a video. There's no way to collect any evidence."

"Except from the house itself, stupid," said Carlos. "We'll just nab some pictures and stuff."

Vanessa really didn't like the idea of that. That was crossing a line.

"I thought you said we weren't taking anything, Ethan," she frowned. "That's stealing."

"We're going to take it back after we show it off," said Ethan with a slight smile. "A picture or something is all we need anyway. It's not like we're gonna steal jewels or anything. Besides, we'll have time to do other things than just look around."

"I hear you there," smirked Lucas. "I don't believe in any of this crap anyway. The only thing I believe in is beer and puss—"

"*Heeeey…*" warned Vanessa. "Keep it clean."

"The princess wants it clean," scoffed Riley. "You're not gonna like it much here, princess. Not at all…Not…at…all."

Vanessa frowned. This little outing was proving to be problematic.

"You may not have a problem with handing yourself out," said Vanessa, "but I like to have something called 'dignity.'"

Riley held up the back of her right hand and wriggled her fingers in Vanessa's face.

"Handy is right," she scoffed again. "You'd know all about that, wouldn't you?...Think you're so perfect…Like you don't give yourself a big fat O."

"Enough, Riles," warned Carlos.

"Yeah," said Lucas. "No cat fights. It spoils the fun…Besides, lover boy wants some of this…"

He squeezed Riley's bottom from behind, and the young lady jumped a little.

"Hey, hands off!" exclaimed Carlos.

He shoved the taller boy away from his girlfriend, but Lucas only grinned at him.

Carlos shook his head and then turned his attention back upon Riley.

"Come on, Riles," said Carlos unhappily. "Stop arguing with Vanessa."

He pushed her forward from behind, but she turned and gave him a disapproving stare.

"I'm not your property," frowned the young Goth woman. "I can take care of myself."

Carlos rolled his eyes and sighed.

"Let's just get on with this," he said firmly. "I want to see what's inside this place anyway."

"And I want to see an empty room," smiled Riley. "You and me can have some alone time. This whole thing is turning me on…"

Vanessa tuned them out. How anything horror related could turn a person on was beyond her.

"Yeah, let's get this over with," said Lucas. "I'm only doing this because I owe Ethan. I'm making that clear right now…Although, I could go for a little alone time with Riles there…"

"Will you cut it out?" demanded Carlos. "Get your own girlfriend."

"I'm game for a threesome," grinned Riley as she looked from Carlos to Lucas and then back to Carlos. "How 'bout it?"

The two boys looked each other over and then shook their heads in a decisive and emphatic "no."

Ethan gave a short chuckle, grinned, and motioned them all toward the abandoned manor in the distance.

"All right, let's go!" he said in vocal excitement. "Come on, we're only wasting time!"

There was nothing more to be said after that. They were doing this whether Vanessa liked it or not, and she most certainly did not like it.

The boys turned off the lights of their respective trucks, and then the five of them trudged toward the house in unison, marching forward like lambs to the slaughter. It was always this way in the movies, a group of teenagers spending the night in an abandoned house…Vanessa really, really did not like this.

Vanessa carried a flashlight with her, a big, black, metal thing Ethan had given her. All of them had one, handed out by Ethan due to his generosity, and that was good, because she seriously doubted this place had lighting or even electricity to run that lighting.

"The old 'spend-a-night-in-the-haunted-house' cliché," said Lucas. "How original."

"You're a walking cliché," scoffed Riley. "You may still be in high school, but you're basically a blonde, college, frat-boy hornball. What would you know about original?"

"I'll show you original when I spear you on the end of my—" began Lucas, but Vanessa would not let him finish.

"Hey, hey, hey!" she said quickly. "I may not get along with Riley, but don't insult her like that."

"Thanks, Mom," said Riley. "I don't need you to defend me."

Vanessa shook her head in response to that obstinance. This was going to be a long night.

They walked up to the double wooden doors, taking one careful step at a time across the old rotting wooden porch.

As much as she hated to admit it, Vanessa realized that there was something to the old 'spend-the-night-in-the-haunted-house' cliché. This place gave her a bad vibe, and that's all there was to it.

The doors were not locked.

Ethan pushed open the doors and stepped inside, so the others followed, but Vanessa was last...She really, really, *really* did not like this.

"We'll leave the doors open just in case," said Ethan quietly.

"You big coward," said Riley.

"Nah, I'm with Ethan on this one," said Lucas. "We'll just leave the doors open for now. We can always close them later."

"Whatever," said Riley in a dry voice.

They shone their lights here and there in what was the living room of this large house. There was old furniture covered with dusty sheets, sheets that had once been white, and cobwebs here and there, but it was the dust, really, that was omnipresent, dust everywhere, dust like a fine layer of silt across the wooden floorboards.

"Talk about abandoned," said Riley. "A whole house just thrown away..."

"Like your virginity," chuckled Lucas.

"Har, har, buttfor," replied Riley. "You're definitely going to be the first to go. I've seen this movie."

"So have I," sneered Lucas. "The Goth girl always gets it, and she always gets it in the worst way."

"And I'm sure you'd like to give it to me," grinned Riley. "Right up the—"

"Will you two quit it?" asked Carlos. "It's getting annoying…and creepy…And speaking of creepy, this place is giving me the creeps, straight up."

"It's just an abandoned house," said Ethan. "There's nothing to worry about."

"It looks like no one has been in here in years," said Vanessa.

"The last disappearance was a census taker in 2020," said Riley.

"That doesn't mean they disappeared here," said Lucas. "They probably stumbled upon a drug deal or something."

Now that was a disturbing thought.

"Do you think any drug dealers could be here?" asked Vanessa.

It was a valid concern. She did not want to be shot for being in the wrong place at the wrong time.

"No, stupid," said Riley. "You just said yourself that no one's been in here in years."

Vanessa did not like to be insulted, but Riley's comment was reassuring, nonetheless.

Vanessa shone her light along the upper railing of a set of stairs. Moving the beam of light revealed an open archway to a kitchen, and she could even see a large, once-white oven in the back.

"There's the kitchen," she said nervously. "There's probably a study or guest bedroom over there, and there's got to be a bathroom on this floor…"

"Good, because I need to go," said Lucas.

"Go outside, you idiot," said Riley. "The plumbing can't possibly work in here."

"Eh, you can leave a couple of floaters," shrugged Lucas. "I don't think anyone's going to care."

"Eww," winced Vanessa.

"Yeah, that is gross," said Riley. "I'd rather wipe my butt with leaves than go anywhere in here."

"I'll get some leaves for you if I get to watch you wipe that big butt," grinned Lucas.

"Double eww," winced Vanessa.

"Yeah, quit it, guys," said Carlos in audible irritation. "You're really grossing me out."

"After all the things I've done to you?" asked Riley. "You've got to be joking..."

"Head in the game guys," sighed Ethan. "Let's focus on what we came for. Speaking of which, we should probably check upstairs...No, wait...Let's check the other rooms first, then head upstairs."

"Sounds good," said Carlos.

"We could always split up," said Lucas.

"No!" said everyone else at once.

They all shared a good laugh over that unified protest. Everyone knew you didn't split up in a horror movie. It was just common sense.

"All right, all right," said Lucas. "Let's cover the first floor."

They took a few minutes to explore. There were four other rooms on the first floor, those rooms consisting of a bathroom, a study with old, moldy books, a bedroom, and a room filled with what looked like exercise equipment. Any furniture was covered by dirty white sheets, but other than that, there was nothing special here.

"There are no pictures, no knickknacks, no nothin'," said Carlos. "There's nothing down here to take with us."

"It's upstairs then," said Ethan. "On we go..."

All five of them trudged upstairs, and there was safety in numbers, but Vanessa was on guard anyway.

The upstairs led to a hallway with three doors on the north side of the house, and those doors led to a master bedroom, a child's bedroom, and a bathroom, but it was the final door on the south side of the hallway that piqued their interest. That door was a solid red, a strange color considering the rest of the whites and browns that cloaked this abandoned house. It was also solitary, just a lone red door in the middle of the south side of this long hallway.

"Last door up here," said Ethan quietly. "We've looked through the other rooms, so let's check out this last one...Huh...Red door...That's weird..."

"After you," said Lucas.

Vanessa did not like the look of this door. It evoked an awful feeling, one of doom on a level she could not describe.

Ethan reached for the doorknob.

"Wait…" said Vanessa. "I have a really bad feeling about this."

"Of course, you do, princess," said Riley.

She pushed past Ethan and reached for the knob.

"Step aside," she ordered.

She rattled the knob, but it would not turn.

"Locked," she said unhappily. "And I really wanted to see what was in there, too…"

Vanessa turned to shine her light upon the top of the stairs. There, in the dim circle-glow of the flashlight, was a little face, a little female face with a pert nose, pixie ears, and big brown eyes staring at her, a dirty little hand on the stained white wall of the hallway, the face of a little girl no older than six staring straight at her.

Vanessa gave a short scream at the sudden scare; she couldn't help it.

The little girl turned and ran down the stairs, her footsteps echoing behind her.

"What the…!" cried Carlos. "Is there someone here! Did you see something!"

"A…A…A little girl…" stammered Vanessa. "She ran down the stairs…"

"It must be a ghost!" said Riley in audible excitement. "We have to catch it!"

Riley bolted past her and took off down the stairs in hot pursuit.

"Whoa, wait, Riley!" yelled Carlos as he took off after his impetuous girlfriend.

Ethan and Lucas immediately followed, Vanessa right behind them, mainly because she did not want to get left behind. She did not want to be alone, not in here.

They hit the bottom of the stairs in a hushed heat, beams of light flashing back and forth. Riley's beam rested upon the little girl, that little girl sitting on the dirty white tiles of the kitchen floor with her back to the oven.

"There she is!" said Riley in strange joy.

Vanessa took a moment to study this new intruder.

This little girl did indeed look to be about five or six, but her state was a rather sorry one. Her clothes were dirty rags, her face was smeared with grime, her hair was long, unkempt, and oily as if it had never been washed, and she was barefoot, the tops of her feet covered with that telltale dirt that only extended neglect could bring. Within her tiny hands, she clutched what was left of a doll, something that had lived long past its due date. Like her, the doll had seen better days.

"It is a little girl…" breathed Lucas.

"I don't think she's a ghost, Riley," said Vanessa. "She must be lost…"

"Oh, yeah?" asked Riley. "Then you go up and touch her. Let's watch your head roll across the floor when she murders the crap out of you."

Vanessa could sense somehow that this little girl was not some phantasm or spirit. This little girl was clearly lost, scared, and probably starving.

"She obviously needs help," said Vanessa. "I'm not just going to walk away."

She slowly walked forward into the kitchen, her hands out as a gesture of peace, but considering this little girl was staring into the flashlights, Vanessa seriously doubted the poor thing could see what any of them were doing anyway.

"Vanessa, be careful…" warned Ethan.

Vanessa ignored him and inched closer to this little lost waif.

"It's okay," she said gently. "I won't hurt you…"

"You shouldn't be here," said the little girl in a quiet voice.

"You shouldn't be here, either," replied Vanessa.

"I live here," said the little girl.

"Who are you?" asked Vanessa.

"Ashley," said the little girl. "That's my name, but that doesn't matter. You're not supposed to be here. You need to leave now, before it's too late."

"Why would it be too late, Ashley?" asked Vanessa.

Now that she knew this lost little girl's name, she was going to use it in order to maintain some calm. She did not want this small thing running off again.

"You have to leave now, before it gets here," said Ashley. "Once it's here, it *won't* let you leave."

"What won't let us leave?" asked Vanessa.

"Knucklebones," said Ashley.

There was a loud snort of laughter from behind her, and Vanessa turned to flash her light upon Lucas's legs, and within that limelight, she could see Lucas's grinning face.

"This is some horse crap!" chuckled Lucas. "You guys set this up to mess with me, didn't you!"

"I didn't set up anything," said Ethan quickly. "Do you honestly think I'd come here by myself?"

"This is nonsense," said Lucas.

"Well, I didn't set up anything," said Riley. "And I can tell when Carlos is lying, so—"

"You *cannot,*" said Carlos. "Don't give me that."

"Look, guys, this is stupid," said Lucas. "Quit this crap."

"I told you, I didn't do anything," denied Ethan.

Vanessa turned her light back upon the little girl, but she received a start, as the dirty little waif was standing right in front of her, right at her feet, staring up at her. The little girl picked up in song after that, a little skip-rope type rhyme with a very simple beat.

"Knucklebones, Knucklebones, nightmare fed…" sang Ashley. "Knucklebones, Knucklebones, under your bed…Knucklebones, Knucklebones, in your sleep…Knucklebones, Knucklebones, your soul to keep."

"That's not creepy at all," said Vanessa in a hushed voice.

"Oh, this is too rich," laughed Lucas. "You've got to be kidding me! This is hilarious!"

"Did you set this up, Ethan?" asked Riley. "This is really hokey. Don't get me wrong, I really appreciate it, but—"

"I didn't set up anything!" barked Ethan. "I don't know who this little girl is!"

This little girl, Ashley, jumped back at the tone of Ethan's voice.

Vanessa turned to address her boyfriend's overt frustration.

"Calm down," she warned. "You're scaring her."

"I am calm," said Ethan, but she could tell he wasn't.

She turned her attention back upon Ashley, but the little girl had changed positions yet again. This time she was over by the east wall, right next to a dust-covered refrigerator.

"It's coming," said the little waif. "It's coming, and it's going to put you in the wall."

"Put me in the wall?" asked Vanessa. "What do you mean by that, Ashley? What do you mean by 'put me in the wall'?"

She did not get an answer, at least, not the one she was looking for. The double doors to the house slammed shut, the doors they had intentionally left open as a precaution, and the slamming of those doors caused Vanessa to turn her attention elsewhere yet again. She spun to shine her light upon the front doors, but Lucas was ahead of her in that respect.

"Hey!" yelled Lucas.

The brash young man ran to the front doors and desperately tried to open them, but they only rattled in place.

"What the…!" hissed Lucas. "The doors are locked! They can't be locked from the inside! It's like they're jammed or something!"

Vanessa shone her light upon Ashley, but the little girl held a new surprise for her. The dirt-smeared waif had opened a panel in the wall next to the fridge, and she was half-in and half-out of a dark tunnel that led to who-knew-where.

"It'll come from under my bed," said Ashley. "You can't get out now. It'll take you one by one."

"Hey, wait—" began Vanessa.

She darted to stop the little waif, but the dirt-smeared child disappeared into the wall as a panel slammed down to shut close from where Ashley had entered.

Vanessa darted forth to open the panel and follow, but there were no seams in the dirty white plaster, nothing to actually open up.

"Wh…What!" she breathed out, but her attention was distracted yet again.

"This isn't funny, Ethan!" yelled Lucas from the living room. "Open the doors!"

"I'm not doing anything!" yelled Ethan in return. "I told you that!"

"Will you two stop!" cried Riley. "We can always smash a window to get out! Now quit fighting."

"We're not fighting!" yelled Lucas and Ethan at the same time.

Vanessa stood and walked back into the living room. She'd had enough of this. They needed to get out of here, and they needed to get out now. Something was definitely wrong, very wrong…She could feel it.

She walked back into the living room just as a quiet descended upon her classmates. Whatever it was they were going to do, she did not know, but she had a more pressing problem than the doors to this house being shut. Ashley had disappeared, and other than just outright vanishing into thin air, the little girl had fled in the creepiest way possible.

"She's gone!" said Vanessa in a slightly-panicked voice.

She had not wanted to sound hysterical, but she was coming off that way, and she did not like it. She did not like anything about this.

"What?" asked Ethan.

"That little girl, Ashley, is gone!" repeated Vanessa. "She opened up a panel in the kitchen wall and disappeared through a tunnel or hole…"

"Ugh…She's like that little girl from *Aliens*," said Riley.

"Aliens? There are aliens now?" asked Vanessa.

"The movie, headcheese," frowned Riley.

"What?" asked Vanessa in complete confusion. "Movie? What movie?"

She had no idea what this girl was talking about.

"Never mind," said Riley in visible disgust.

Vanessa wanted to say something in return, something nasty, because Riley was really getting on her nerves, but Lucas prevented that from happening. The blond young man ripped a dusty white sheet from a small wooden stand, picked up the aging piece of furniture, and walked toward the nearest window, the one closest to the east wall.

"Hey, wait!" yelled Ethan, but Lucas ignored him.

The young man hauled back and tossed the piece of furniture at the window with all his might. The old wooden stand simply bounced off the glass and hit the floor with a loud clatter, breaking apart as it did. There wasn't even a scratch on the glass for his efforts.

"Son of a…" hissed Lucas.

He took his heavy metal flashlight and swung full force with it at the window in question. The flashlight bounced off the glass like a rubber ball hitting the floor, and he was thrown backwards to land on his butt upon the dust-covered wood.

"What the…!" cried Lucas.

Vanessa's heart raced out of control. She was beginning to feel like this was no trick, like this was no practical joke that Ethan or any of the others had set up beforehand.

"Sh…She said it was coming for us," stammered Vanessa. "She said Knucklebones was coming for us, and that it wouldn't let us leave. She said it would come out from under her bed."

Lucas hopped to his feet and gave her a stare that would have peeled fresh paint.

"Oh, yeah?" he asked. "Well, I got something for him…I'm gonna go give it to him right now!"

He slammed his flashlight down into the palm of his left hand and pushed past all of them. He started up the stairs, and the others followed, so once again, Vanessa was forced to follow as well.

"I don't know who you got to come here, Ethan," warned Lucas, "but I've got something for him. This is on you."

"I didn't do anything, you idiot!" yelled Ethan. "I've got nothing to do with this! I told you that!"

"Oh, yeah?" asked Lucas. "Tell that to the dude whose skull I'm about to cave in."

The young man tromped through the upstairs hallway to the child's room, opened the bedroom door, and walked in without another word. Everyone else showed up at the entrance to the room, but Carlos stepped inside as well, Ethan right behind the other two boys.

Vanessa stood by Riley at the doorway as everyone shone their lights around the small room to look for anything, anything at all.

The child's bedroom consisted of a small bed covered with a dirty white sheet, a small bookcase with time-ravaged children's books lining it, a couple of dressers, some old toys scattered here and there, and what looked like a tall lamp covered by a ragged black sheet.

"Come on out, Knucklebones!" cried Lucas. "I got something for ya!"

"Be careful, Lucas!" warned Riley.

There was a tension in her voice, something a little more than passing concern. Vanessa wondered if there was something going on between the two teens, Lucas and Riley, but such a thought was ridiculous. Lucas only dated college girls.

Lucas stepped into the center of the room, visible anger upon his face, visible even through what little lighting they had.

The young man spun in a circle, flashing his light here and there, and then he knelt as he inspected the underneath of the small children's bed. He stood and turned, backed up, and thumped his flashlight twice in the palm of his left hand.

Vanessa could not help but stare behind Lucas; she could not help but stare at the tall lamp covered by the ragged black sheet. She could not remember it being in here when they had inspected the room the first time.

"That wasn't there before…" she whispered.

"What?" asked Riley. "What wasn't there?"

But with nothing else to find in the room, Lucas turned his rage upon his friends.

"There's nothing in here, Ethan!" he spat. "I'm tired of this game, and I want out of this hole! Now unlock the front doors so we can leave!"

"I told you already, you stupid…!" began Ethan, but his angry voice trailed off as he stared behind Lucas.

Vanessa watched in stationary horror as the so-called lamp in the ragged black sheet began to move behind Lucas, rising as if by magic…It was clearly no lamp at all.

Two long and spindly skeletal arms emerged from underneath the black sheet as the slender figure grew even taller, at least seven feet in height. Large skeletal hands opened up at the ends of those arms as those arms stretched forth, those arms opening wide to an uncanny five feet in length each, the span between the hands insane for any normal person. Two more boney arms appeared from underneath the black sheet, just under the first two, and two more large skeletal hands opened up to spread forth with equal menace. It was like watching a spider unfold its legs, though there were only four arms, not eight legs.

"Lucas!" screeched Riley.

Lucas turned and shouted as he swung his flashlight in self-defense.

The creature caught the heavy metal tube with its upper-right hand, and then it crushed that light, the plastic lens breaking, the metal tube folding in on itself as if the act of breaking a tactical flashlight were nothing. It dropped what was left of the crushed light to the floor, the pieces scattering across the dusty wood below.

Lucas tried to back away as all four skeletal arms grabbed him at once.

He was quickly bent backwards, the sound of his spine snapping in an echo around the small room, and then he was folded in half as he was picked up by massive strength a moment later, bloody spittle shooting from his lips in an arc.

The creature folded him like a dinner napkin after that, breaking his legs forward at the knees, breaking his arms backwards at the elbows, folding him into a square as Lucas's dying, blood-choked shrieks faded out within seconds.

Vanessa screamed…They all did.

They all ran a moment later, all of them in unison, all down the stairs and to the front doors, the doors that were locked and would not budge.

Carlos ran to the front doors along with Ethan, and both of them struggled to turn the knobs and pull at the doors to open them.

"Help! Help!" cried Carlos.

The two boys banged on the doors over and over again until Ethan switched to a window and started hitting it with his flashlight, but nothing gave. They were trapped, and they knew it.

“There’s gotta be a way out of here!” cried Ethan.

“Lu…Lucas!” cried Riley. “It killed Lucas!”

Her voice was a high-pitched whine, and Vanessa could see tears in the Goth girl’s dark eyes. Vanessa had not expected this kind of reaction from Riley, as the young woman had always been brash and somewhat obnoxious about almost everything.

The young Goth woman ran past Vanessa and entered the kitchen. Vanessa followed her, because she was following Riley’s logic…There had to be a back door.

The dark-haired Goth girl ran to the singular back door at the south-west wall of the kitchen, that door a dirt-smeared gate of white wood with an old brass doorknob, but try as she might, this door would not budge, either.

“No, no, NO!” yelled Riley as she banged on the door with her flashlight. “Let me out!”

“There has to be another way out!” cried Vanessa. “Come on!”

She bolted from the kitchen to find the boys, but they were not difficult to locate. They were still banging on the front doors and the windows, but to no avail.

Right now, she needed to be the voice of reason, because everyone else was in a full panic.

“Everyone, stop!” yelled Vanessa. “There has to be another way out! There has to be a basement, or an attic, or something with a broken window! This house has been abandoned for years! There has to be something broken we can crawl through!”

“Yeah…Yeah, that’s a good idea,” huffed out Carlos.

“Are you nuts!” cried Ethan. “Do you really want to go into the basement of this place!...And we can’t reach the attic without going back upstairs!”

“We have to do something!” argued Carlos. “We can’t just wait around to get murdered by that thing!”

“She said it would pick us off one by one,” said Vanessa.

“It…It killed Lucas…” said Riley in a choked voice.

Vanessa turned to inspect the Goth girl, but Riley was a weeping mess, her eyeshadow running down her cheeks in black trails.

"Yeah, it got Lucas…" said Ethan in a haunted voice. "We'll have to tell people after we get back to town, but first we have to…we have to get out of here."

"It killed L…Lucas…" repeated Riley in a quickly-breaking voice.

She broke down into loud sobs as she wept into her hands.

Carlos walked over to her to put his arm around her shoulders, but the young woman threw off his hand in a strange fit.

"What?" asked Carlos. "Babe?"

"I loved him…" wept Riley.

"What?" asked Carlos in confusion, but that confusion quickly turned to rage.

"What!" yelled the boy again, only this time with angry force.

"We were seeing each other…" choked out Riley. "I was going to tell you…"

"What!" yelled Carlos a third time.

He pulled back his right hand and then backhanded her, the sound of the blow loud and audibly painful in the forced silence of this terrible place.

Riley shrieked as she fell to the floor, and Vanessa was at her side in a heartbeat, even as Ethan was pulling back an enraged Carlos.

"Chill, man!" yelled Ethan. "You can't hit a girl!"

Carlos struggled against him as Ethan wrestled him from behind.

"She's not a girl!" yelled Carlos. "She's a whore!...Let me go! Get off me!"

Vanessa pulled Riley to her feet, and the young Goth woman held her right cheek where she had been struck.

Riley was still a weepy mess, but Vanessa gently lowered the girl's hand from her cheek. Vanessa was not fond of Riley, but the sight of the quickly purpling bruise upon the young woman's previously unblemished skin enraged Vanessa to no end, and that rage was directly squarely at Carlos.

"Don't you ever hit her again!" she screeched.

Her outburst stunned the two remaining boys into silence. It was not like her to go full fury, not at all, so for her to show such primal emotion was both new and shocking.

A few seconds passed before Carlos brushed off Ethan, straightened his letter jacket, and walked away from them all toward the front doors.

"You don't defend her," he said in a low voice. "You don't defend that no-good cheating whore."

"You can't hit her man," said Ethan as he shook his head no. "I know she cheated on you, but you can't hit her. It's not cool."

"She's a WHORE!" shouted Carlos.

He stepped forward and pointed an accusing finger at Riley as the young woman choked out a sob and hid her bruised face within the confines of Vanessa's pink jacket.

"She's lucky I don't kill her," said Carlos. "I should just leave her for that thing upstairs."

Riley choked out another sob, and Vanessa put her left arm around her for some small comfort.

Vanessa glared at Carlos, not that such a look would change anything. He was a jealous, abusive scumbag as far as she was concerned.

Her boyfriend, however, was the voice of reason this time.

"Don't say that, man," said Ethan. "You don't want that…You know you don't want that…All of us need to get out of here anyway. You're just gonna have to shove this down deep and forget about it for now. We don't have time for that. We gotta get outta here first."

Carlos whined and palmed himself in the face a couple of times. Vanessa could see his eyes tearing up, and the young man drew in a choked sob at the same time.

"You gotta get it together," said Ethan. "We have to get out of here. We'll talk about this once we're out of this place. At this point, I'm even willing to go down to the base—"

He never got to finish his sentence.

Ethan was standing by a small circular table, part of what had to be a spillover of dining room from the kitchen, a half-choke of rooms that had simply been merged for convenience, living room and dining room in one setting. The table in question was covered by a dust-caked white sheet, that sheet hanging down to the floor, and it was from beneath that sheet that two skeletal hands on long, boney arms reached forth and grabbed Ethan by his ankles.

Ethan was pulled to the floor, falling straight down, dropping like a weight as the creature attacked. He cried out as he was dragged underneath the table, but to Carlos's credit, the jilted young man grabbed onto Ethan's outstretched hands, though it did little good.

Vanessa shrieked along with Riley as Ethan screamed, the young man's scream an audible wrack of terrible pain. Blood flew from Ethan's lips in synchrony to the sounds of bones snapping, his body half-in and half-out from beneath the table sheet, and even though Carlos had ahold of his friend's hands, and even though Carlos leaned back with all of his weight to pull, his sneakers on their heels, Ethan slipped from his grasp and disappeared beneath the table in one last, high-pitched, agonizing wail.

Carlos fell on his rump as Ethan was pulled from his grasp. The young man immediately hopped to his feet, swiveled, and gave the two girls a crazed, wide-eyed stare.

"GOOOOO!" he shouted.

Vanessa had to drag/pull Riley toward the kitchen. The weight of her own boyfriend's sudden death had not dropped upon her, not yet, not like it had with Riley on the death of the girl's lover, but it would, and she knew that. Right now, she had to get out of this house.

She pried open the basement door in the kitchen and shone a light down the rickety wooden stairs leading below. There had to be some way out of this house, either up or down, and she was going to find it.

But the only thing she found was grief, and she was crying by the time she landed feet first at the bottom of the stairs, even as she dragged Riley along with her. That grief had hit her sooner than later.

"It killed h…him…" she choked out.

Riley nodded in understanding. They at least had that in common.

The door to the basement slammed shut as Carlos leapt down after them.

"We gotta get outta here now!" he ordered, but truth be told, neither Vanessa nor Riley were in any shape to do anything, and Vanessa knew that.

"It killed Ethan…" she choked out. "It…It dragged him under the table…"

She sobbed into her hands as that emotion threatened to drown her, but she did not get to grieve for long.

Carlos pried her away from Riley and slapped Vanessa across the left cheek with his right hand. The blow stung, but Vanessa could do nothing but stare back at him in surprise.

"Snap out of it!" he commanded. "We don't have time for this!"

"Leave her alone!" sobbed Riley. "Don't hit her!"

Carlos released Vanessa and immediately grabbed the Goth girl by her right wrist with his left hand. He raised his right hand to strike her, and Riley immediately flinched, but the young man's right hand never came down with that punishing force.

"AaaaAAAGH!" shouted Carlos. "You whore!…Oh, I should…I want to…Ugh…Get away from me…You're not worth it…"

He shoved her away and shook his head in disgust.

"I don't have time for this," he said angrily. "I've gotta find a window or something. There's got to be something we can squeeze through."

He shone his flashlight around the basement, an active attempt to actually be helpful, so Vanessa wiped at her own tears and searched as well, shining her light here and there to look for any kind of a way out.

There was nothing down here but an old washer, an old dryer, and the rotting wood of an old workbench with some rusty tools on it. Other than that, this large cement block of a basement was bare, just a huge rectangle of old sewage smells and water stains.

Carlos walked forward and picked up a rusty machete from the workbench. He took a couple of swings with it, determined that the handle would not snap off, and continued to shine his light here and there.

This was a problem, of course. Vanessa did not want the young man armed. He was just as likely to kill them as that thing upstairs. She did not want her head hacked off in a jealous rage.

She picked up a rusty icepick and slipped it to Riley. The young Goth woman took the weathered tool and hid it behind her back.

Carlos stamped around in a circle, shining his light about him, but his frustration was visible even before it was audible.

"There's nothing down here!" he yelled. "There's no way out!"

Vanessa shone her light around the basement and realized he was right. There were no windows down here, just the ceiling, the floor, and solid concrete walls.

"I told you," came Ashley's voice from behind them.

All three of them turned and shone their lights on the dirt-smeared little girl.

"It won't let you leave," said Ashley.

"It's the ghost…" said Riley in a low voice.

Vanessa stepped forward and grabbed the little waif by the shoulders. In spite of what Riley believed, Ashley was solid, corporeal, and she was warm to the touch. Vanessa could feel the little girl's breath on her face as she knelt down before her.

"She's not a ghost," said Vanessa. "She's just a scared little girl."

"Oh, yeah?" asked Carlos. "Then what's she doing here? How did she get down here?"

Vanessa ignored him for the moment. She shoved her grief down and concentrated on escape, escape for all of them, and Carlos's hostility wasn't helping. She needed to get out of here and tell someone about Ethan and Lucas. They deserved that much, but she needed some answers first, and she sensed that this lost little girl had those answers.

"How did you get here, Ashley?" she asked.

"I live here," said Ashley.

"You live in this dump with that thing?" asked Riley in audible disbelief.

Vanessa did not know how this little girl could possibly live here, but she was distracted by the marks on Ashley's arms. She pushed up the ragged right sleeve of the shirt Ashley wore, its colors long since faded, and she winced at the sight of old scars, scars that looked like cuts and burn marks.

"Who did this to you, Ashley?" asked Vanessa in angry disgust. "Who hurt you? Did Knucklebones do this to you?"

"Kind of," said the little girl in a flat voice.

"Kind of?" asked Riley. "What the…? What in the hell does that mean?"

Vanessa continued to ask the important questions, because if Ashley actually did live in this terrible place, then the little waif had to know of a way out.

"Where are your parents?" asked Vanessa. "Do you know where your mommy and daddy are, Ashley?"

Ashley pointed up toward the ceiling with her right index finger.

"Knucklebones," she replied.

Vanessa felt a chill seep straight down to her core. Whatever was going on here was beyond her, beyond all of them, but she was not giving up. There had to be a way out, and Ashley was the key to that escape…but Vanessa's questioning was sidetracked by Riley.

"Three travelers disappeared," said the young Goth woman in a haunted voice. "I don't know the exact details, but a couple disappeared four years ago. They must have had a kid with them."

"How old are you, Ashley?" asked Vanessa.

The little girl simply shrugged.

"She's got to be five or six," said Riley. "That means she was a toddler at the time…Then that means…"

"That means that thing has been taking care of her," said Carlos in a panicked voice. "That's what she is! She's bait!"

"What?" asked Vanessa in confusion.

Carlos pointed the tip of his rusty machete at Ashley's smudged face.

"She's bait for that thing!" he accused. "She'll lead it right to us!"

Vanessa glared at him in warning. The distraught young man was becoming crazier and crazier by the second.

"She's not bait, you psycho!" she hissed. "She's just a scared little girl!...I don't know why that thing hasn't killed her, but…look at what it's done to her!"

She pulled up the rags of Ashley's shirt and showed off the burn marks upon the girl's pale, dirty belly.

"Then she's its toy!" exclaimed Carlos. "That's what she is! It just keeps her around to torture her…"

"Which is why we have to get her out of here!" yelled Vanessa. "We're not sticking around long enough for that thing to come find us and kill us, and we're sure as hell not leaving Ashley behind just to get tortured!"

Carlos stroked back his black hair with his left hand, his dark eyes wide as his mind visibly worked out some thought on the matter. He let forth a little whine as his eyes misted over with tears, a working of emotion that was visible even in the dark.

"I…I don't…I don't know what to do…" he said in a choked voice.

"We gotta get outta here," said Riley in a wavering voice.

"Yeah…Yeah," nodded Carlos. "That's…That's it…That's what we gotta do…"

Vanessa turned her attention back upon the abandoned little girl.

"Listen, Ashley," she said in a firm voice. "We have to get out of here. You have to know a way out."

The little girl nodded once in understanding.

"Does that mean you know a way out?" asked Vanessa.

Ashley nodded once more, and Vanessa sighed in relief.

"Why haven't you left then?" she asked. "Why didn't you try to find help, Ashley?"

"Grownups are scary," said the little girl in a flat voice. "Knucklebones puts them in the wall."

"Puts them in the wall?" asked Riley. "What does that mean?"

"It means she's a little psycho," nodded Carlos. "We can't count on her…but there has to be a way out. There's gotta be. It's got to be in the attic of this place. It's gotta be…But first we gotta ditch this little creep. She's bait for that thing…"

"We're not leaving her," warned Vanessa. "And you need to calm down. You're not helping."

"I need to calm down?" asked Carlos in disbelief. "I need to calm down! That thing is going to be here any second!"

"Stop it!" warned Vanessa again. "Stop it now, or I'll…I'll…!"

She stood up and moved Ashley behind her, and Carlos immediately brandished the machete, waving the rusty tool in her face.

"*You* better stop!" he said angrily.

"Put the machete down," said Vanessa in a wavering voice. "Put it down, or I'll…I'll kill you. I won't let you hurt a little girl."

In truth, she felt like peeing herself, but she held in her visible fear, though she was shaking inside.

Carlos cocked his head to one side and gave her a look of death. She could see a certain finality in his dark eyes, a cold fire burning within those orbs that was impossible to ignore.

"You'll kill me, huh?" he said quietly. "You want me to put this down, huh?...Oh, I'll put it down…"

He gave her a strange grin, an awful and tangible malice brimming beneath it, something that instantly froze her in place.

"In fact, I know just where to put it," he said in a weird voice.

He lifted the rusty blade high as Vanessa's eyes followed the makeshift weapon. The old tool was poised to come down and bury its rusted blade right in her forehead, right between her eyes, but she was frozen, petrified at that moment, her death imminent.

The blade began its descent, but it never reached its destination.

Carlos cried out as he dropped the rusty weapon he had been holding in his right hand, the machete clattering upon concrete as it hit the floor. He staggered backwards as he reached back and held his left side with his left hand, his eyes squeezed shut, his face wracked with sudden pain.

Riley stood there with her flashlight in her left hand, her right hand wrapped around the handle of the rusty icepick, the browned tip of it coated with fresh blood.

Carlos turned to look at her with hurt in his eyes, a deep hurt that was so tangible it could be felt from a distance.

"Baby…?" he asked.

He staggered backwards a couple of steps as Riley let out a low sob, her eyes welling up with tears once more.

"I'm sorry!" she whined.

Vanessa had no thoughts running through her head as she shone her flashlight upon the injured Carlos. This particular scenario had never once crossed her mind.

If Carlos was going to say anything more, he never got the chance to.

Two long and spindly skeletal arms reached forth from the dark behind him, those skeletal hands gripping him by the head, and two more long and spindly skeletal arms shot forth as well, those white fingerbones gripping him about the waist. He was bent backwards after that, his neck snapping along with his spine as his head was pushed down to touch the small of his own back.

The sound of Carlos being brutally murdered was like a loud snapping of twigs, or maybe small branches being broken in half, but whatever the case, that sound of breaking bones was enough to jolt Vanessa out of her fear-induced helplessness.

"NOOOO!" screamed Riley, and Vanessa's body moved as if on command.

"RUN!" shouted Vanessa.

She turned to grab Ashley, but the little girl was already gone, already across the expanse of the empty basement. The orphan waif was half-in and half-out of the west wall, once again escaping through a square hole in the wall, a square hole in solid concrete, a square hole that Vanessa was certain had not been there before.

"This way," mouthed the little girl, but whether she had mouthed it or spoken it, Vanessa could not tell, as Riley's scream was still echoing in her ears.

Vanessa dragged Riley forward toward this new exit as more sounds of snapping bones echoed around this empty concrete basement. They practically fell over each other as they followed the little girl into the small, dark tunnel in the west wall, but follow they did, and without hesitation.

It was a tight fit for them, but Vanessa still had her light, and Riley still had hers, so they crawled in a straight line over dirty stone or concrete after the leading form of little Ashley, their lights bobbing here and there in this basement underdark.

Ashley traveled about thirty feet in a straight line through this underground tunnel, but Vanessa could tell that this so-called escape route only led to a blank black wall and nothing more.

"We're trapped in here!" said Vanessa in a panic.

"No," said Ashley.

The little orphan waif pressed against the flat black before her, and a panel slid open to reveal an intense light, a brightness so pervasive that Vanessa had to close her eyes for a second in order for them to adjust.

The little girl before her crawled through the opening and into the white area the opened panel had revealed. Vanessa quickly followed her, crawling out of the hole, only to stand in a large room of pristine white, bright round bulbs embedded in ivory plaster above them, those lights shining down upon this empty, blisteringly-white room.

Riley crawled out of the hole last and stood, her tear-strewn face a mask of surprise, her dark, weeping eyes wide from the shock of these new surroundings.

This new room was empty save for two very important features. The first feature was the red door in the center of the north wall, a red door identical to the red door Vanessa had seen upstairs, only in reverse, the doorknob on the right side of the door rather than the left.

"This must be the room with the red door…" she said in a hushed voice. "But that's impossible!…We were in the basement, and the red door's upstairs…"

The bright red of the door surrounded by the stark white of the rest of the room had distracted her, for she had not noticed the second feature of this room, that is…not until Riley let out a high-pitched whine of sheer emotional agony.

Vanessa turned to address the young Goth woman, but the second feature of the room thoroughly stole her attention away from Riley's emotional outburst.

The walls were lined with faces, faces molded of plaster, each with the defined detail that only a master sculptor could bring.

Riley stood before one particular face embedded within the wall, the face of her now dead lover, Lucas. His particular molding was at Riley's head height along the wall, a little over five feet up from the shiny, white-tiled floor, and that face held a permanent look of shock and pain, as if he were in a physical agony to match Riley's emotional one.

"L...Lucas..." choked out the Goth girl.

There were eighteen faces in all, and there were fifteen strangers all in various facial expressions of shock, horror, and pain, those first fifteen faces strung out across the east and south walls, but the last three were on the west wall, and Vanessa knew them well.

Her tears flowed as she walked over next to Riley in order to study Ethan's face. Her own dead boyfriend's face was right next to Lucas's, and the look on Ethan's face, his mouth open, the lips curled back in a terrible scream...

"Ethan..." wept Vanessa.

Even Carlos was here, his face in the wall, though how that thing had put him in here so quickly, Vanessa could not fathom.

"This is where the grownups are kept," said Ashley in a quiet voice.

"This is..." choked out Vanessa. "This is upstairs, Ashley. We were in the basement...All we did was crawl in a straight line...How did we get up here?"

She turned to stare down at the little girl, her mind unrealistically expecting some kind of intelligent answer, but the dirt-smudged orphan waif in rags simply shrugged her little shoulders in reply, a blank expression upon her dirty face.

Vanessa turned and studied the other faces permanently locked within the wall, but something rose to the surface of her mind, something that instantly bothered her.

"There are fifteen other people in here," she said as she struggled to wipe her eyes free of tears. "Fifteen people have disappeared over the last thirty years...so...what happened to the original family? Where are they? There should be two more adults and a child…"

Both she and Riley turned at the same time to stare at Ashley. Vanessa figured the both of them were thinking the same thing, and that thought was highly unpleasant.

"How long have you been here, Ashley?" she asked.

The little girl shrugged again, the same blank expression upon her face as before.

"Where are your parents, *Ashley*?" asked Riley, and her voice was not kind.

Alarm bells rang in Vanessa's head as the young Goth woman pushed past her to stand before the strange child of this abandoned manor. Vanessa could clearly see the bloody icepick hidden in Riley's right hand, but she could not fathom why Riley would suddenly wish harm upon this helpless little girl.

"*Where* are your *parents*, Ashley!" asked Riley once more, this time with an audible viciousness that was undeniable.

"Kn…Knucklebones," stammered the little girl. "Knucklebones…"

"What are you doing?" demanded Vanessa as she stood between Riley and Ashley.

She was not about to let this little girl suffer one second more. Riley had suddenly gone off the deep end, and Vanessa would not allow her to hurt Ashley.

"Move out of the way, princess," said Riley in a threatening tone. "This has to be done…"

"What has to be done?" asked Vanessa. "What are you talking about?"

"This thing is bait for that thing," said Riley in rising anger. "Carlos was right…Don't you get it?...She's the little girl from the family that disappeared thirty years ago…She's the little Faerber girl…She has to go. She has to die."

Vanessa pushed Ashley backwards and toward the east wall. One glance backwards, however, revealed that there was no open panel, no open hole to escape through. There was only white plaster, seamless, no sign of any means of the passage or tunnel they had escaped through.

Nevertheless, Vanessa was not about to let Riley hurt Ashley.

"She's just a little girl!" she exclaimed in her own rising anger. "Leave her alone!"

"She's been here for thirty years, Vanessa," warned Riley. "She's never aged a day…She's been here for thirty years, and she's never aged a day…You know she wasn't with one of those travelers from out of town…There would have been a record of a little girl missing along with them…I knew something was funny about that the moment I first suggested it…The only record of a missing little girl is the Faerber girl that disappeared thirty years ago."

"Wha…What about Missy Carlyle?" stammered Vanessa. "She disappeared three years ago…"

"Her mom ran off with her because her dad won custody," said Riley. "Everybody in town knows that."

The young Goth woman's voice was becoming more and more strained, more crazed.

"Now move out of the way," warned Riley. "I mean it…This thing got Lucas killed, got Carlos killed…She even got your own boyfriend killed…She summoned it, you know. She summoned it with that rhyme of hers…

"Knucklebones, Knucklebones, nightmare fed…I remember the words…Knucklebones, Knucklebones, under your bed…That's how it goes, doesn't it?...Knucklebones, Knucklebones, in your sleep…Knucklebones, Knucklebones, your soul to keep…

"That's what's in the walls, Vanessa…It kills you, and then it traps your soul in the walls…She brought it to us…She did this…She killed Lucas…She killed Lucas, and now she has to die…Now…Now, move out of the way, or I'll kill you too."

"She can't be that Faerber girl!" cried Vanessa. "The Faerbers probably moved away! They'd be in the wall otherwise!"

"They probably are in the wall," said Riley in a deadly serious tone. "It's possible not all of the vanished people ended up here…I'm telling you…she's the Faerber girl…I know…I know it. I can feel it. There's something wrong with her, princess…I can tell. We were in the basement, and now we're up here…That's not normal. She's the Faerber girl, and she's been here for thirty years. She hasn't aged a day. She hasn't aged a day, and that's not normal."

"Nothing about this is normal!" yelled Vanessa. "Can't you see that? You can't hurt her, Riley! She's just a lost, starving little girl that's been tortured…"

"She's bait for that thing," said Riley in a cold voice. "It's just like Carlos said. She's bait for that thing, and she got Lucas killed…Now move out of the way, Vanessa. It's time to end this."

"You can't do thi…!" started Vanessa, but her voice trailed off as she watched the red door behind Riley open in a slow, silent, inward swing.

"I won't say it again," said Riley, her voice low and tinged with madness. "Move out of the way, Vanessa."

"R…Riley…" stammered Vanessa.

The creature entered the room on gnarled, bony feet. Riley sensed its presence and turned, her face twisting in terror at the skull face looking down upon her.

Vanessa could clearly see its face now. This Knucklebones' face was nothing more than a skull and two dull white orbs where its eyes should have been. She could see a reddish tongue in-between its grinning teeth, its jaws creaking open as its four arms spread forth from the black rags it wore as a sheet over its narrow, skeletal frame.

"No…No, wait…" said Riley in a high-pitched voice filled with terror.

This terrible thing gripped her around the waist and lifted her up into the air to bring her face to face with its own grinning skull. It opened its jaws and screeched, a loud, shrill, and piercing call that reverberated around the white room, temporarily deafening Vanessa by sheer magnitude of sound.

"W…Wait…I…I'm sorry," choked out Riley.

The creature turned her over and laid her across its two lower arms while holding onto her with its upper-left hand. It raised its upper-right hand high into the air as if to spank her, and all the while, Riley begged for mercy.

"I'm sorry, I'm sorry!" screeched the young Goth girl. "Please, please, STOP!"

This horrible wraith brought down its skeletal right hand, and the fingerbones plunged into Riley's back, right through her black leather jacket, right in and through her black shirt.

Blood spurted up in a fountain from the horrible wound, spraying everywhere in a red stream. Riley's body stiffened as her mouth dropped wide open in shock, her eyes rolling up into half-whites, her legs stiff and shaking from the vicious assault. The creature then gripped Riley's spine right above her tailbone, and then it pulled up, ripping upwards with one horrible, hideous motion.

Vanessa nearly passed out at the sight of it, this bloodbath of carnage on formerly spotless white.

Riley's entire skeleton was pulled forth from her flesh, that flesh dropping to the floor like a bloody, empty meat sack of skin, muscle, and tendons, her empty face folding in on itself and plopping backwards with no skull to give it shape, the eyes snapping off at the optical nerves to spill away from the bloody flesh shell. Multiple organs spilled from the female skeleton—intestines, stomach, liver, heart, lungs—to splatter across the bloody meat sack below.

This creature, Knucklebones, dropped the gore-soaked skeleton to the flesh pile below and held up a ball of blue light in its bloody upper-right hand. That strange, unearthly light flew from its skeletal fingers and embedded in the wall, right next to Carlos's face.

Vanessa wept and let forth a whining sob as Riley's face formed in the plaster of the wall, that face desperately trying to speak, but no words could be formed from its alabaster lips. Riley closed her eyes as black tears spilled down her stiffening cheeks, and then she was nothing more than a white plaster face with a trail of black under each closed eye.

Vanessa backed away toward the east wall as the creature stepped forward on long, boney legs. She put herself in-between Ashley and the terrible wraith…If she were going to die, she was going to make sure Ashley got away.

The creature bent down to look around and behind Vanessa, but she would not allow it a solid view of the little orphan waif.

"You can't have her," said Vanessa in a low voice.

She spread her arms wide as the creature tried again to peer around her in a futile attempt to look upon the little girl.

"You won't hurt her anymore!" yelled Vanessa.

This creature, this "Knucklebones," spread all four of its arms wide, leaned forward, unhinged its jaws, and let forth its unholy screech.

A terrible wind blew about Vanessa, her hair flying about her face, and she had to momentarily close her eyes from the gale force of it. She was going to die, and she knew that, but she was not going to die in vain.

"Run, Ashley!" yelled Vanessa. "I'll protect you!"

The hideous shroud of bones before them stood up straight and tall as it prepared to strike, but its attack did not come, not yet.

Vanessa felt a tugging at her pink jacket, and she looked down with wide, panicked eyes into the dirt-smudged face of the hapless waif.

"You'll protect me?" asked Ashley in a quiet, sad voice.

"Yes!" said Vanessa in a panicked rush. "Now get out of here! Go through that tunnel! I know you can open it somehow! Go through it and get out of this house! Run away from here! Run far, far away! Run as fast as you can!"

The little girl let go of her jacket and then turned toward the giant, skeletal creature threatening them.

Knucklebones lurched forward to grab Vanessa, but those terrible, boney hands never reached her.

"No," said Ashley in a quiet voice.

The creature staggered backwards as if struck by an invisible blow, its grinning jaws opening slightly as if in surprise.

"No, Mommy," said the little girl.

The horrible wraith in black rags screeched yet again as it staggered backwards a few steps more.

"No, Daddy," said Ashley.

This terrible nightmare from the depths of insanity staggered backwards until it reached the west wall, the wall with all of Vanessa's friends' faces, the wall where those friends were trapped for all eternity as far as Vanessa understood.

Vanessa watched in both surprise and shock as little Ashley pointed one dirty finger at Knucklebones.

"You're bad," said the little girl. "You hurt me…You burned me, Mommy…You hit me, Daddy…You were supposed to protect me…but you didn't…I don't want you here anymore…Her name's Vanessa, and she's nice…She'll protect me now."

The creature laid flat against the wall, its four arms spread, its jaws wide open as it let forth one last piercing shriek.

"It's time for you to go into the wall," said Ashley.

Vanessa lips parted in a gasp as the creature melded into the wall, melding until its body disappeared into the plaster, melding until the black rags vanished into white, melding until there was only a plaster skull left, a plaster skull with white orbs for eyes.

Vanessa knelt down, grabbed Ashley by her little shoulders, and spun the little girl around.

"How did you do that, Ashley!" she asked. "How did you do that!"

"I don't know," shrugged the dirt-smudged waif.

"I…I…I don't understand…" stammered Vanessa. "Was that thing your parents? Is that where your parents went?"

The little girl gave her a slow nod in reply.

"What happened to them?" asked Vanessa. "Why were they like that? How did they become Knucklebones?"

"They hurt me," said Ashley in a quiet voice. "They were monsters…"

"Monsters?" asked Vanessa.

"They hurt me," repeated Ashley. "They didn't protect me, so I made sure they would protect me forever…"

Vanessa's heart leapt into her throat. A terrible thought had come to her, something so awful she could not quite comprehend it, and yet comprehend it, she did.

"Did…Did you do that to them?" asked Vanessa in growing horror. "Did you make them into Knucklebones?"

"They hurt me," repeated Ashley.

"But…But all those people in the walls…my friends…" said Vanessa as more tears came to her eyes. "Why?...Why would you do that?"

"Grownups are scary," said the little girl. "They're mean…Knucklebones made sure they couldn't be mean…That's why they're here."

"Oh, my God," said Vanessa with wide, tear-filled eyes. "R…Riley was right…"

"You're nice, and you're pretty, like my dolly," nodded Ashley.

Vanessa wept into her hands as she tried to make sense of it all, but it all felt so senseless now, so terribly meaningless.

She lowered her shaking hands and placed them upon Ashley's little shoulders.

"Do you understand what you've done?" asked Vanessa. "Do you even understand what's happened here!"

The little girl nodded and smiled.

"You're going to protect me now," she said firmly.

Vanessa felt a pain in her chest, and she clutched her pink shirt and jacket as she winced in sudden physical torment. She fell backwards onto her bottom as more pain washed over her, a torture that spread throughout all of her limbs as well.

"You're nice, and you're pretty," repeated Ashley. "Just like my dolly."

Vanessa cried out as pain wracked her entire body. She shivered and shook as a strange sensation ran through her, an unearthly feeling as if she were being overwhelmed by some otherworldly force.

"You'll protect me now," repeated Ashley. "That makes me happy."

Vanessa stared down at the fingers of her left hand. The pain in those fingers was slowly going away, but now they felt stiff, and with good reason…They looked like plastic.

She raised both hands and let out a low whine as she gawped in wide-eyed horror at her new plastic hands. She reached up with those plastic fingers to feel her stiffening face, but her cheeks felt just as cold, hard, and lifeless as the rest of her.

"You're so pretty," smiled Ashley. "See?"

Vanessa looked up and saw her reflection in a large mirror on the south wall, a mirror in a pink wooden frame, a mirror that had not been there mere seconds ago.

She was a human-sized doll now, a mannequin with oversized eyes and red, red lips, her skin a shiny peach plastic, her joints stiff and difficult to move. She was terrifying in that uncanny-valley sense, something that would have scared her to no end if she had seen it in a movie.

"I'll call you 'Doll Face'," said Ashley in a happy voice. "You can protect me now. You're much prettier than Knucklebones, and I can comb your hair…That makes me happy."

Vanessa tried to speak, but no sound escaped her plastic lips. She could only turn her head and move in a very stiff manner, and try as she might, she could not stand up.

Ashley stretched her little twig-like arms above her own head and yawned.

"I'm sleepy, Doll Face," said the little girl. "Carry me to bed…You can sleep in my bed with me."

Vanessa stood and was compelled to do as commanded. She could not fight this overwhelming feeling, could not fight the sheer force of will that worked against her own meager version of such.

She reached down, picked up Ashley with ease, and balanced the little girl on her left hip. She then exited the white room through the red door and carried the little girl to the child's bedroom, her gait a stiff march, her plastic limbs brimming with a new, unnatural strength.

"You'll protect me from now on," smiled Ashley. "When more grownups come, you'll put them in the wall now."

Vanessa's horror ballooned out of control as she laid her new charge down on the dirty white sheet of the child's bed.

The weird, warped little girl stared up at her with a happy smile.

"I love you, Doll Face," smiled Ashley. "But we have to make up a song for you now…The words come to me when I think about it, and I don't know what they mean sometimes, but I'll think about a song right now, 'cause you need one…Let's see…How about…Oh, I know…How about…Doll Face, Doll Face, in the night…Doll Face, Doll Face, giggling fright…Doll Face, Doll Face, pay her toll…Doll Face, Doll Face, takes your soul…"

Vanessa now understood the true meaning of horror.

*****

George was beginning to regret coming to this abandoned house, but he had Mickey, an idiot, true, but reliable, and he had Geena, his girlfriend, so it wasn't like he was here alone.

They'd come here to nab some stuff and sell it, but the prospects of finding anything of worth in this dump were swiftly looking null.

"There's nothing in here," said Mickey.

George scanned the living room area with his flashlight one more time before waving the beam of light toward one of the side rooms.

"Check the other rooms like Geena, then," he ordered. "There's gotta be something of value in here. We can't just keep stealing copper to make a few bucks. We need something more substantial."

"Yeah, yeah," said Mickey. "Don't I know it. I'd like an eight ball of meth."

"That stuff eats your brain," said George. "I just wanna do something nice for Geena…Take her to dinner and a show…That reminds me…Where is she? Her sweet butt has got to have found something by now."

There was a clicking of high heels as their third companion walked out of the dark of one of the side rooms.

"Speak of the Devil," said George in frustration. "Where in the hell have you…"

He shone his beam upon her, but his voice trailed off as he stared at his girlfriend and partner in crime. She stared back at him, but she had backed out of the room she had been in, her own light facing the wrong way, so it was impossible for her to be staring at him…except for the fact that her head was twisted all the way around on her neck.

She fell, quite dead, onto her back to land face first as two large plastic hands reached forth from the darkness to grip her ankles and pull her body back into that black void.

George sucked in his breath in horror as a large plastic face appeared out of the dark and into his beam of light, a moving mannequin of a young woman dressed all in pink, her face beset with large brown eyes and red, red lips, and then that terrifying face disappeared into the darkness of the other room, but not before sounding out a haunting girlish and bubbly laughter.

#2...THE LIGHT RUNNERS

Out of the frying pan and into the fire.

Shane sat down at the long steel cafeteria table with the others. This cafeteria was not very large as such, and it only had one table, but the table itself hosted all thirty participants with ease.

This was Aaron Cordon's facility, so it was a mix of expense combined with practicality. The billionaire made sure they had what they needed, but without any extras. Shane likened the man's character to a spoiled twelve-year-old with way too much money, but that was the personality of billionaires; they didn't live in the real world...Not that it mattered much. Shane would never get to meet the man.

His stomach rumbled as he winced from the starving feeling trying to pull out his guts and play skip rope with them. Everyone here had been taking Cordon's new drug for the last week, and Shane didn't know about the rest of the participants, but he felt as if he'd just been run over by a truck. He was starving, tired, and just plain ill from whatever was in that new drug.

But that was why he was here. He was getting paid two grand for this glorified sleepover/Guinea-pig experiment, so as long as he didn't die or start losing limbs, it was all worth it for the cash.

"Oh, I am ready to eat a horse," he mumbled.

"I hear that," said Quarron, a young, twenty-one-year-old black kid from Georgia. "I'm ready to eat two."

The young man sat across from Shane, Quarron sitting down on one of the many round metal stools that curved up from underneath this steel table.

Quarron picked up the shiny, chrome-colored, juice-type pack in front of him and pulled off the plastic straw glued to the side of it. He punched a hole in the top of the container with the straw's pointed bottom tip, and then he took a sip, a look of slight surprise on his young face as he tasted what he was drinking.

Shane didn't particularly have a problem with Quarron, although the kid could really talk his ear off at times.

"Mmm," smiled Quarron. "This is good. Can't wait for some actual food, though."

"No kidding," grunted Shane.

Shane was a big man of thirty-six, six-foot-two in height, broad-shouldered, and lined with natural muscle from years of working construction and farm work. He was indeed a big man, and he knew that some people didn't quite understand the fact that big men needed to eat. Except for the first two days they'd been here, all they'd had over the last week were small red cakes for food, dried disks that looked like dark-red urinal cakes, and that crap was sustaining, but it wasn't satisfying. In fact, Shane wondered if this generally-ill feeling plaguing him was from simply not eating enough.

Shane picked up his juice-pack, tore off the straw, and punched a hole in the top of the chrome-colored container. He took a sip, and the liquid flowing into his mouth automatically perked him up, though not as much as he would have liked. This juice had an odd taste, something he could not quite define, but at this point, he didn't care…It would do for now. He had been promised real food today—they all had—and that was why he was here right now with the other twenty-nine participants. Everyone wanted to eat.

"Where are the vittles?" asked Bart, an older man in his late sixties.

The old man sat down next to Quarron and longingly stared at the empty space where food should have been.

Bart had been around the block and then some, and he was kind of funny once you got to know him. He had that sense of humor that only old people tended to have, always dated but somewhat amusing.

"This is all we got so far," said Quarron. "Just this weird juice and nothing else. I'm really hoping we get steak, though. I need something to really sink my teeth into."

"I normally can't have red meat," replied Bart, "but after a week of those crap-cakes, I wouldn't mind a big fat steak. I wouldn't care if it was mooing at me."

Shane snorted out a slight laugh. Leave it to Bart to make him feel better.

Donna walked up and sat next to Shane. She was a couple of years younger than him, and she was fairly attractive—long brown hair, hourglass figure, decent boobs—but he wasn't interested in any women right now. He'd already had one disastrous marriage under his belt, and that divorce had finally gone through earlier this year. He wasn't ready to hop back in that saddle.

He could tell, however, that she stuck close to him because he looked like an alpha male. He had a rugged face combined with short black hair, a short black beard that wrapped around to his hairline, and a black mustache that circled down to his beard. Combined with his size, he could easily model for one of those romance book covers…Women were attracted to that brawny look for some reason. She probably saw him as a natural leader, and he could take that role when necessary, though he did not like to.

"I am so ready to eat," breathed Donna. "I can't wait to get some real food…and my clothes back."

She was dressed in a light-blue one-piece, the same blue outfit they all wore, cut to size, of course, that outfit just a loose-fitting garment of a long-sleeved shirt and pants coupled with black socks and black heel-cut outdoorsman boots. The only thing that differentiated their clothes was a number, a big number in black print over the left breast. Donna's was #12.

"They wouldn't even let me have a bra," said Donna. "I don't even have any underwear."

"We're all going commando," snorted Quarron. "And we're not even allowed to have sex…It was in the contract. Get caught doing the nasty, and you're out. You don't get paid…Seems like kind of a waste to me. There are some hotties here."

Shane rolled his eyes. Sex was the last thing on his mind right now. No, right now he just wanted to eat, and he wanted to eat some real food, not the "crap-cakes" Bart had coined as such.

Two children walked up and filled the remaining two seats. There was Adrian, who was eight, a quiet little boy who never had much to say, and Zuri, who was six, a little chatterbox of a girl who never stopped talking, at least, not when Shane was around.

Zuri sat down by Donna, and Adrian sat down next to Bart. That was all thirty of them now at the table, all thirty of them ready and waiting to be fed some real food.

"They said we get to have real food today," said Zuri. "I can't wait. I want fish and spaghetti. That's my favorite."

"Fish and spaghetti?" asked Bart. "You're supposed to eat spaghetti with meatballs and fish with tartar sauce."

"I like fish with spaghetti," replied Zuri. "My mom always makes fish on the side. I like catfish, though. It's my favorite fish to eat."

"Well, you got good taste there," smiled Bart.

"Where's the food?" asked Adrian.

"Food's coming, I'm sure," said Bart. "You just have your juice now, youngin'. That should tide you over."

The two kids prepared their juice containers and took sips from them.

"This tastes funny," said Adrian.

"I like it," smiled Zuri. "I think it tastes good."

"You think everything tastes good," frowned Adrian.

Zuri stuck out her tongue at him, and Adrian stuck out his tongue in return. Quarron barked out a short laugh over the exchange, and this gave Shane a slight smile.

There were little moments here that made Shane feel like he was part of a family, and that feeling was rare considering the hard life he had led.

"Well, we only have to be here a couple more weeks," he said after a moment of thought. "After that, we can all go out to eat or something. I wouldn't mind having a goodbye party. You folks are really the only ones here that I've gotten to know anyway."

"That's a great idea!" said Donna happily. "I wouldn't mind Mexican or Chinese..."

"Burger for me," nodded Quarron. "I like Mexican and Chinese, but I really want some meat for some reason."

"Yeah…" said Donna with a thoughtful look. "I really could go for a double cheeseburger right now…That's weird, too. I'm mostly a vegetarian. I normally don't like too much meat."

"Works for me," said Bart. "Hamburgers it is."

"Done and done," smiled Shane.

They all sipped away at their drinks after that, letting a couple of minutes pass as they finished their juice containers. The other twenty-four participants prattled on and chattered away as people do, but Shane's little group remained quiet for the moment.

He had not been in this cafeteria before, and in fact, except for taking short trips to a medical lab, he had not been out of the dorm area where the study participants were housed. None of them had, so Shane took this quiet opportunity to study his surroundings.

This small cafeteria was basically a metal box of chrome flooring and black metal walls.

They had all entered through the west side where the dorms were located, but he was more interested in the two large sets of double doors on the east side. He did not know where they led, probably to more labs, but that was no surprise if they did.

In-between those two sets of double doors was a huge flatscreen, one that spanned the entire wall, something he just now noticed. It was basically the size of a cinema screen, so maybe they were going to get to watch a movie in here. That would definitely be nice.

There was a singular door in the southeast wall, but that was probably a service door that led to the kitchen, so he had no interest in that.

Above him was an expanse of twenty feet to the ceiling, that ceiling a flat, black-metal roof with fluorescent lights beaming down from above, those lights set in-between huge metal slats that were designed to open inward, though for what purpose they opened, he did not know.

In fact, this whole setup was weird. He'd never seen any building designed like this, not in this depressing, futuristic, dark-metal and shiny-chrome look. It was like a mix of Goth and science fiction. All he could figure was that Aaron Cordon's taste in architecture was odd.

He thought about this for a few seconds, and then Bart looked as if he were about to say something, but the old man never got to speak what was on his mind. The enormous flat screen on the east wall lit up, and everyone's attention was diverted toward that.

A man sitting at a chrome desk in a stark white office appeared on the screen, and Shane recognized him immediately…It was the billionaire himself, Aaron Cordon.

The billionaire tech mogul—and apparently a pharmaceutical genius now—was dressed in a plain black T-shirt, no suit and tie, nothing to pin him as the rich fancy pants everyone knew him to be. He had a punchably-smug grin on his face, and Shane found his distaste for the man rising even before their "generous" host had uttered a single spoken word.

"Greetings, my little Guinea pigs!" said Cordon in a cordial tone.

There was slight laughter amongst the crowd gathered here, but Shane didn't care about that. He just wanted to know what was up. He wasn't sure if this was a recording or a live feed, but he couldn't imagine that a billionaire dink like Aaron Cordon would even give them the time of day…It had to be a recording.

"As you know, you've all been gathered together for a groundbreaking experiment," continued Cordon. "You've all been injected with Serum #463, and if you're wondering where the control group is…don't. There is no control group."

Shane's little group of six was sitting on the east side, the very most end of the east side of the table, so they were closest to the screen and the two sets of double doors, which, in retrospect, was why Bart's comment was overheard at all.

"Well, that's not very scientific," muttered Bart.

"Right you are, Mr. Stanford," nodded Cordon.

There were gasps in the crowd as everyone realized the same thing…This was a live feed. "The" Aaron Cordon was actually live on the screen before them, and he even knew their names…Well, he knew Bart's name anyway.

Cordon clapped his hands together and rested his elbows on his desk. He had a huge grin on his punchable face, and Shane could tell the man was amused at the reaction of the plebeians before him.

"This isn't about science," said Cordon. "No, this is about progress…You see, Serum #463 has the ability to greatly prolong the lifespan of the recipient. It stops the aging process. You can heal wounds in minutes that would take days to heal, and you can even heal serious injuries in days that would take months to heal."

There were excited rumblings amongst the crowd, and Shane could understand their enthusiasm, but he wasn't buying it. There was no fountain of youth formula as far as he was concerned. Besides, he'd felt like crap all week long, and if feeling like this was what it took to stay alive longer, then he wanted no part of it.

The billionaire on the screen parted his hands, rested them back upon his desk, and then screwed up his lips in visible thought.

"There are some unfortunate side effects," he said after a second. "This is why I haven't personally used the serum, but we've tested it four-hundred-and-sixty-two times, and #463 is definitely a winner. All results on our test animals have proven to be excellent with run #462, so naturally we moved on to human beings."

"Wait…" spoke up a man at the other end of the table, someone Shane did not know. "Is this F.D.A. approved?"

Cordon laughed and then shone forth that huge, irritating grin of his.

"Oh, Mr. Lewandowski, we don't have the time to go through the government," he said quickly. "No, there's no need to worry about that."

The cafeteria erupted in both angry and fearful protests, but Shane kept his mouth shut. He was brimming with anger now, that rage building up, but there would be plenty of time for lawsuits and whatnot after he got out of this facility, and he was leaving today, payment or not.

The billionaire waved his hands in a downward motion for silence, and the crowd in the cafeteria reluctantly acquiesced.

"I specifically scouted and chose each and every one of you because of your unique status in society," he nodded. "All of you are in financial trouble in one way or another, except for the two children up here in front, Adrian and Zuri, who come from poor, underprivileged families. All of the rest of you, in essence, are dirt-poor adults with no prospects, no futures, no retirement savings—welfare parasites—pretty much the losers of society, and that's why you're here."

"What are you saying!" cried out another man that Shane did not know.

"I'm saying, Mr. Ackles, that the real test begins now," smiled Cordon. "You were all expecting to eat a real meal today, and you will, but only if you make it to one of the Finish Rooms. You see, whoever makes it to a Finish Room will immediately be hired onto my staff with a starting salary of two-hundred-and-sixty-thousand a year."

All complaints and anger died with that single statement. There were loud gasps and excited bursts of verbal joy, but Shane did not feel any of that enthusiasm. Something was not right here, something was off, and it was the fact that Cordon had stated, "whoever *makes* it to a Finish Room." That sounded ominous, and Shane did not like ominous.

"Everyone, calm down!" said Cordon in a loud voice. "Everyone, calm down, please!"

The cafeteria crowd quieted, and the man on the giant screen gave a short smile.

"We'll get you hired on," he nodded. "However, I only allow intelligent people on my staff, intelligent and driven people, so you actually have to make it to a Finish Room in order to be hired on. You need those two traits, intelligence and drive, in order to work for me."

He clapped his hands together again and grinned, that grin Shane could not stand. Cordon then lowered his head slightly and narrowed his dark eyes in a look that Shane did not like at all, one he liked even less than that smug grin. The expression made Cordon look like a snake about to strike, and Shane would not have been surprised if the man's skin just peeled off to reveal scales underneath.

"Now, the rules are simple," said Cordon in a predacious tone. "You just have to make it to one of the Finish Rooms. You can use any of the doors up front here, but the paths to the Finish Rooms are all different, so be warned."

"Warned about what?" asked a woman at the other end of the table, a rather fat white woman in her thirties.

"Sloth, Ms. De Luca," replied the billionaire. "I expect results, not lollygagging. You need to hustle and be smart enough to make it to a Finish Room. Once you do, you'll have a real meal waiting for you, and we'll get you hired on…If you don't make it…well…you're disposable."

"What?" asked Donna in a slight gasp.

Shane could tell she was thinking the same thing he was. "Disposable" was another word for "dead."

"What does that mean!" yelled someone else in the crowd, another man that Shane did not know.

"That's a popular question, isn't it?" smiled Cordon. "It means I don't have a use for the poor and stupid, Mr. Gerbach. You can be one or the other, but society doesn't need both…Now…I suggest you start moving. Once the first shutter opens, the doors will unlock, and once the shutters open…well…I would start running. Otherwise, your cremations will be pretty quick."

The cafeteria erupted in protests of rage and fear yet again, but the soulless scumbag on the giant screen simply grinned at them.

"Good luck!" he said in a sadistically happy tone, and then the screen went blank, that giant screen returning right back to the former ebon wall it had been.

Shane cursed under his breath. Unless this was some kind of messed-up psychological experiment Cordon was pulling on them, everyone in here was in real danger.

"Son of a…" he started. "We've got to get out of here."

"What's going on?" asked Quarron. "Is this for real? What did he mean by 'cremations'?"

The young man's face was a mask of fear and anxiety.

"Can't say for sure," said Bart with a grim frown. "All I can say is that we better take him seriously."

"What should we do?" asked Donna, her voice tremulous with that same tangible fear as Quarron.

Shane thought about this, but he did not have to think for long. He noticed the little service door out of his left peripheral, the service door he had completely ignored before, and a plan quickly formed in his mind. He was no longer going to ignore that door.

"We head for the single door," said Shane. "Cordon said we could use any of the doors up front. I'm thinking we should hit that little service door up there."

The group turned their heads to stare over at the singular, so-called "service door."

"That's our best bet," said Shane. "Cordon wants intelligent people, so I'm thinking a herd mentality will head for the double doors, right or left, doesn't matter. I've seen cattle stampede without any kind of direction before, so trust me…those double doors have to be the wrong way, or they're tougher paths to follow than that little door. Either way, I think the right choice is that service door. Let everybody else take the double doors."

Quarron turned and gave him a worried frown.

"That's cold, man," he said unhappily. "That's cold, but I understand where you're coming from."

"Unfortunately, he's right," grimaced Bart.

"But all of these people…" trailed Donna.

"It's either us or them," said Bart, "and we have two children with us. I hate to agree with Shane, but he's right. If anything, we have to do it for the kids."

"What if it's not the right way, though?" asked Quarron. "We could be screwing ourselves ov—"

He was cut short as a loud clang occurred at the other end of the cafeteria.

Shane watched in cold silence as the first of the black-metal shutters opened up on the ceiling at the opposite end of the table, those shutters falling open to stream in a bright light that shone upon the cafeteria floor directly next to the entrance and exit to the doors that led to the dorms.

"It's started," said Shane.

Donna gripped him by the arm, an instinctual reaction, he knew, born out of fear.

People around the table began to stand, and some of them walked forward toward the double doors, but some of the people at the end of the table were still talking and not moving. There was plenty of excited, angry, and fearful chattering, but not much in the way of reaction to the first open shutter.

Shane stood and motioned everyone else to stand, and his little group reluctantly did so.

"What are these fools doing?" asked Bart. "They should be getting their butts in—"

Like Quarron's previous comment, the old man's statement was destined to never be completed.

The next shutter opened, and light came pouring from the ceiling over the first section of table nearest the dorms.

The fat woman who had spoken earlier, Ms. De Luca, was standing at that end talking to another male participant Shane did not know, but as the light shone down upon her, she simply cried out in a loud, shrill, and agonizing scream. Her fat, pale face blackened as it charred over in the light, and then she burst into flames, her whole figure going up in a pyre, a blazing pillar of orange and blue.

The man talking to her caught fire as well, though only half of him had been standing in the light. He screamed as well, though he staggered a few feet as a living column of flame before collapsing to the chrome-like floor.

"OH!" shouted Quarron, just before the screams around them began.

The rest of the cafeteria burst into chaos, a mass of people running, shouting, and screaming as they practically trampled each other in a rush for an exit.

Shane's mouth dropped open at the black stain on the shiny floor, that section of floor that gleamed from the light shining down from overhead at the opposite end of the table. Ms. Deluca was now nothing more than a black stain, not even clothes left behind.

The deceased man that Shane did not know the name of was still burning, but his body was collapsed on the floor outside of the light. It was clear that direct exposure to the light was instantly fatal, but in order to completely incinerate someone…the source of that light had to be a weapon more powerful than Shane had ever heard of. They could not afford to get caught in it.

People rushed past their group as they stampeded towards the double doors, and Shane cursed himself for being right about their herdlike mindlessness. He had not wanted to be cold and ruthless by not warning people about the double doors, but his own little group had two children in it, and he did not want their little bodies to go up like lit matchsticks.

But any guilt could wait. Right now…they needed to run.

"We'll be like ants under a magnifying lens!" yelled Shane. "Everybody, move, now!"

The next shutter opened just as he finished his desperate command.

There was no more room for discussion. Shane swept up Zuri in his arms while Bart took Adrian by the hand, and all six of them headed toward the singular "service door."

Zuri whined in Shane's ear as Quarron pulled open the service door and ushered them inside.

"Come on, everybody!" cried Quarron.

They filed into a narrow hallway, and the first thing Shane did was look up. This narrow hallway also had a tall ceiling and shutters lining that ceiling, but those shutters were smaller than the cafeteria shutters, these particular shutters set acrost the width of this hallway, each one designed to open after so much time had passed.

"Don't stop moving!" grunted Shane as their group filed into the hallway.

They fled down that hallway to the next door. They crowded around that singular door at the end of the hallway, and Quarron was already tugging on that door, but the door barring their exit would not budge.

"I can't open it!" cried the young man. "It's locked!"

"Now, wait just a minute," said Bart. "Let's not panic…There's something on the wall here."

The wall on their left contained three, small, flat touchscreens, those screens lit up with questions that apparently had to be answered.

There was a loud clang as the first of the shutters in this hallway opened, and then light came streaming in to blaze upon the floor next to the door at the other end, the singular service door they had originally passed through.

"Hurry!" warned Donna. "It's starting in here!"

Shane took a brief moment to look over the three screens, and each one contained a different question.

"We have to answer these questions," he grunted.

The first one was a math question, an equation that looked like gibberish to Shane. Math was not his strong suit, but maybe someone else had the answer to this one.

The second question was multiple choice, something about three farmers in a field and how they could work together in order to produce a shape that would maximize their crops, and although Shane had worked on farms, this also looked like math…He'd come back to it later.

The third question was not so much a question but a shape of some kind, and the question beneath that shape was simply "WHO AM I?" There was an answer line on the screen underneath that question with a touch keypad underneath that…He was afraid this one was going to be impossible to answer.

But he was wrong.

"Oh, it's Gerbilon!" said Zuri. "That's Gerbilon!"

"What?" asked Shane in confusion.

He turned to look at Zuri's face; he'd forgotten he'd been holding her. She was staring at the last screen, the one with the odd shape.

Adrian stared at the shape as well before nodding once.

"Yep, that's Gerbilon," said the little boy.

"What's a Gerbilon?" asked Bart.

"It's a Collecto Monster," said Zuri. "You know, like Burnamole."

"I have no idea what that is, little one," said Bart.

"It's that kids show and card game," said Quarron. "Collecto Monsters…It's where different cutesy monsters battle it out and—"

The next shutter opened with a loud clang, and more light lit up the shiny chrome of the hallway. They were running out of time, and quickly.

"Quick!" cried Donna. "Just type it in! That'll be one question out of the way!"

"I don't know all the monsters!" hissed Quarron. "I don't know how to spell it!"

"G-E-R-B-I-L-O-N," spelled out Adrian.

Quarron quickly punched in the letters and hit enter. There was a loud click as the door directly in front of them unlocked. Quarron tugged at the handle, and the door swung inward.

"Snagged it!" he said excitedly. "We just needed to answer one!"

"Everybody, through the door!" commanded Shane.

They entered the next room, and the floor in this room was just as narrow as the previous hallway, but this time there was a pit on each side of the floor, or the floor was a bridge, rather. Their floor was now a bridge that spanned a large gap, spanning a pit that sank down about thirty feet, and at the bottom of that pit were flames, roaring flames that meant a terrible death for anyone falling into them. In fact, the heat from below was so intense that Shane instinctively backed away, but he knew he couldn't go backwards…There was no turning back.

He looked up at the shutters above him and realized that their time in this room was limited in more ways than one.

"It's hot!" yelled Zuri.

"How are we supposed to cross this!" replied Quarron. "This room is a death trap!"

They were all standing at the beginning of this new room, half-in and half-out of this large square chamber, but one look back the way they came revealed the next shutter opening, so there was no time for debate.

"They're all death traps!" barked Shane. "We've got to cross anyway!"

Bursts of flame erupted from several holes in the floor a few feet ahead of them, then a few more feet ahead, and then those spouts of flame erupted down the bridge, then in the middle of the bridge, and finally they erupted right next to their little group.

Donna shrieked and backed away.

"What do we do!" she screeched. "We can't cross that!"

"That rich sucker is intent on roasting us!" hissed Shane. "Damn him!"

"Give me a second!" cried Quarron. "Just give me a second…"

The young man watched the bursting flames with an intensity that confused Shane, but Quarron's study of those flames paid off a few seconds later.

"It's a pattern!" said the young man in excitement. "They're bursting in a pattern! I know, because I play a lot of retro video games. I can tell you when to move—"

"Good!" barked Shane. "We'll get the kids across first. Donna, you take Zuri, and Bart, take Adrian next."

"Got it," said Bart. "Donna, honey, you should go first with Zuri. Adrian and I will be right behind you."

There was a loud clang from the hallway they had just exited.

"There's no time!" cried Quarron. "Just go! This bridge is just wide enough for two people at a time! That means Shane and I will go last!"

Shane lowered Zuri to the floor, and Donna took the little girl's hand in her own, but Zuri struggled against her.

"We can't go through that!" screeched the little girl.

Thankfully, Donna proved to be the levelheaded one this time.

"We have to," she said quickly. "We have to, honey. That light's going to burn us up if we don't. Do you understand?"

"Y…Yeah…" said Zuri.

"Quarron will tell us when it's time to go," continued Donna, "and then he'll tell us when we have to stop, okay?...Can you do that?"

Zuri looked back at the light streaming down in the hallway they had just left. She looked up at Donna a second later, her swarthy little face ringed with fear, but she nodded in compliance.

Donna looked toward Quarron and nodded once.

"When do we go?" she asked in a heated rush.

The flames burst ahead of them in a pattern, and Shane tried to memorize it, but Quarron was way ahead of him.

"Go!" said the young man.

The pair of females stepped forward just as the next shutter opened in the previous hallway.

"And stop!" ordered Quarron.

Donna held Zuri close to her as spouts of flame burst right in front of them. The bridge was narrow, but Shane had faith that Donna would not allow Zuri to fall.

"Go!" said Quarron.

"It's hot!" yelled Donna.

"Keep moving!" yelled Shane in return.

The pair walked forward until Quarron barked at them to stop. Their journey forward did not last long, however. The young man's instructions safely guided them until Donna and Zuri had stepped beyond the last flame trap and were standing before the next door.

"Bart and Adrian, you go next," ordered Shane.

The old man nodded and took Adrian by the hand, leading the little boy forward according to Quarron's instructions. They crossed safely moments later, and it was a good thing they had, because the last shutter in the previous hallway opened behind Shane and Quarron.

"We have to move now!" yelled Shane.

But the spouts of flame upon the narrow bridge burst at their own speed.

"Give it a second…" said Quarron. "Now!...And stop!"

Shane stepped forward along with the young man just as the first shutter of this room opened to blaze down that incinerating light from above. He could feel a radiance from that light, an aura of something he could not describe, something he immediately recoiled from. Whatever this radiation was, it was more than just light, and whatever *that* was…it was deadly.

"You're cutting it close!" cried Shane. "Cordon's trying to fry us with some kind of laser!"

Quarron ignored him and gave the next order to move.

"Now!" he said. "And stop!"

They continued in this way until they rejoined the group, but Donna had already opened the next door.

"Come on!" she said as she motioned them onward with her left hand.

They stepped into the next room as a unified whole. Whatever was going to happen, they were now a united front, and that was good, because Shane knew they needed all hands on deck in order to outrun Aaron Cordon's deadly race against time.

The next room was a large square that looked empty at first, but appearances were deceiving when it came to anything in this insane facility.

Quarron stepped forward, and Shane could tell that the young man was only moving forward in order to give people more space, but alarm bells rang in Shane's head, so he laid one big right hand on the young man's right shoulder to keep him from moving.

"Wait!" he said quickly. "We don't know what this room is about…"

He did a quick scan of the floor. This room's floor consisted of eight rows of six large metal plates in each row. They had entered the room and were standing on a simple line of chrome flooring, that flooring safe and unmarked, but then the rows of plates began, and each plate outside of the starter line of flooring was lined with flame spigots; Shane immediately recognized those deadly spouts.

Each of the floor plates was a shiny chrome color, each large enough to allow three to four people standing room, and each plate had a single huge letter engraved in them, each letter different, the first row of plates consisting of "S, L, P, T, O, and E."

"This must be some kind of anagram," said Shane as he scratched his head. "I'm not good at these."

"I am," said Donna as she stood next to Shane. "Each row has the same letters, just in different orders. Once you get to row five, however, it switches to numbers."

Shane looked up and winced once more at the closed shutters lining the ceiling.

"Cordon must love fire, because these plates are boobytrapped," he grimaced. "Step on the wrong one, and you're hit with the flames. Stick around too long, and the light incinerates you. That must be why all the floors are so shiny. Helps reflect the light."

"That's great, but we need to solve this right now," said Quarron. "There's no time to screw around."

"Any ideas?" asked Shane. "Anyone?"

"Oh!" said Donna as her face lit up with excitement. "I have it!"

"Already?" asked Bart. "That was fast."

"I'm good at these," grinned Donna. "Anyway, this particular anagram spells two words that come to mind regarding our current situation. They are 'STEP' and 'LOSE.' So the first four plates we want to step on are…"

She walked over and hopped onto the plate engraved with a large "S" before Shane could stop her, but thankfully, nothing happened. No flames erupted from the floor, and Donna was not turned into a living pyre.

Shane breathed out a sigh of relief over this, but this feeling of relief was quickly replaced by worrisome anger.

"Will you give us some warning!" he barked. "Don't just march forward like that! You could have been killed!"

"Sorry," said Donna with a sheepish grin.

"It doesn't matter right now," said Shane as he shook his head. "Just be more careful from now on…Anyway, let's keep moving…Everyone, follow Donna!"

The thirty-four-year-old woman jumped from the "S" plate to the "T" plate that was diagonal from her original position, and once again, nothing happened. She was not burned to a crisp, and Shane was thankful for that.

She walked from the "T" plate to the "E" plate, and then from the "E" plate to the "P" plate, only stopping before the new plates with numbers on them. Everyone followed her lead, the two children on Donna's "P" plate and the three men right behind her on the "E" plate.

"Wait a second, everyone," she said unhappily. "I don't know what these numbers mean."

The first of the shutters in this room opened with an echoing clang, and this sparked immediate haste in Shane.

"We need to figure it out, and fast!" he warned.

"I don't know what the numbers mean!" cried Donna in return. "They don't make any sense! There's no mathematical anything to base them on!"

Shane stared at the line of numbered plates that made up the fifth row. Those numbers were "8, 5, 4, 18, 1, and 20," respectively. Those numbers repeated as the letters had, but in different orders for rows six, seven, and eight, just like the differing orders of the letter plates the group had already passed.

Of course, like Donna, he did not know what he was looking at, but fortunately, Bart knew the answer to this puzzle.

"They're letters," said the old man. "They're just the numerical orders of them, their numbers in the alphabet. Learned that when I was in the Junior Detective's Club when I was in grade school. You see, you have, from left to right, '8, 5, 4, 18, 1, and 20'. That equals 'H, E, D, R, A, T'."

"Hedrat?" asked Quarron. "What does that spell? Because we're gonna be dead rats if we don't get out of here fast."

"Exactly," said Donna. "I think 'DEATH' is one of the words. The other one is 'HERE', which must be the safe word, because the whole room puzzle answer would be 'STEP HERE'…Plus, you know, four plates to step on. 'DEATH' would be five plates, so there you go."

"'HERE' would be plates '8, 5, 18, and 5'," said Bart. "'8, 5, 18, and 5. Follow that order."

"Good enough for me," said Shane. "Step back, Donna. I'll go first just in case."

The next shutter opened, this one above the second row of the room.

"Move!" yelled Shane. "There's no more time!"

Donna quickly switched places with him, and he stepped onto the "8" plate diagonally right from his position on the "P" plate. He breathed out a sigh of relief and then motioned the kids forward. Quarron, Donna, and Bart followed right behind them as Shane checked the remaining three plates while moving the kids forward directly after each safety check.

With Donna and Bart's help, they had found the correct path through this room, and they reached the next door without further incident, but this didn't stop Shane from complaining. He was way past sick of this.

"How many of these rooms are left!" he hissed.

He stepped into another long and narrow hallway, this one at least five times longer than the original hallway they had entered. This hallway was surrounded by chrome metal walls and a chrome metal floor, and it was only wide enough to fit two people at a time.

He picked up Zuri, and Donna led Adrian by the hand beside her, the pair of them behind Shane. Quarron and Bart walked behind Donna and Adrian as all of them filed into this new, unknown, amorphous threat.

"It's another hallway," said Shane. "Be ready for anything."

He walked forward along with the others, but the moment all of them had traveled past the beginning of this straight shot, loud clangs occurred in the previous room as the shutters in that room dropped one after the other.

All of them turned to watch as the first shutter in this hallway opened, and then the next opened five seconds after that.

"It's not stopping!" yelled Shane. "RUN!"

Shane dashed forward with Zuri in his arms. Quarron picked up Adrian and huffed it beside Bart as Donna ran in-between the two groups.

The shutters opened one after the next behind them as they dashed to the end of this hallway, that deadly light streaming in with each newly-opened shutter, that light that would incinerate them all if they could not open this new door.

They hit the last door at full speed, and written in large red letters upon that door were the words, "SPEAK THE TWO TRAITS NECESSARY TO WORK FOR ME, AND YOU MAY ENTER." Upon the left wall next to the door was an intercom lit with two large, red, rectangular lights.

"Two traits!" exclaimed Quarron. "Uhhh…What were they?…Oh, wait…OH!...Intelligence!"

The first of the red lights turned green as the shutters continued to open down the hallway, those shutters making a quick beeline for them all. They were all huddled around this door, this frustrating barrier between death and another chance to live, but they only needed one more correct answer to open said door.

"What was the other one!" cried Shane.

"It was…It was…" stammered Donna. "Being driven!...Drive!"

The second light flipped to green, the door unlocked, and Shane practically ripped open the door.

All of them piled into the next room as the door behind them shut and locked again.

Shane quickly studied his surroundings, his mind automatically focused on searching for the next exit.

This room was just a small white room with white walls, a white ceiling, a white tiled floor, and a large flatscreen monitor mounted upon the wall opposite of the locked door they had just passed through. Beside that monitor was a singular white wooden door with no means to open it, no handle to pull or knob to turn to get them into the next room.

"What the…!" huffed out Shane as he lowered Zuri to the floor. "There're no shutters in here!"

"That means…" said Donna quietly. "That means…we made it?"

"I sure hope so," said Quarron.

The screen upon the wall opposite of their little group lit up, and the smiling face of Aaron Cordon appeared before them. The sadistic billionaire clasped his hands in front of himself, his elbows on his shiny desk, and then he grinned like a Cheshire cat, an expression none of them wanted to see.

"Congratulations!" said Cordon with strange zeal. "You've won! You even took the single door, which means you skipped an entire room for that little bit of ingenious thinking. Good job! That means my staff will begin the paperwork to get you started right aw—"

"Now, hold on just a minute!" yelled Shane.

Cordon did not seem surprised at this outburst and interruption. He simply shrugged, smiled, and waited for whatever Shane was going to say, and Shane definitely had a few words for him.

"You can't just use some kind of crazy weapon on us and expect us to be friendly!" yelled Shane. "You tried to kill us! You've murdered two people already, and who knows how many of the other trial participants have died in the other rooms!"

"You tried to fry us in those rooms!" yelled Quarron. "You can't just test out some kind of new laser weapon on us!"

"I have heard the sun is a deadly laser," shrugged Cordon. "I think that's a meme or a song or something…"

"This isn't a joke!" cried Donna. "You've murdered people!"

"And I can still dispose of you right now, Ms. Bendel," said Cordon as he screwed up his lips in pensive thought. "If you like, I can just have security come in here and kill you all."

"Wh…What?" asked Donna.

Shane studied Donna, but her face was extra pale at this point. Her condition was probably fear mixed with shock, and that was compounded by adrenaline mixed with just plain overexertion. It had to be, because that was what he was feeling.

Whatever the case, it was clear that Cordon held all of the cards here, so Shane did not know what to do, but the old man behind him stepped forward and replied for all of them.

"Now, let's not get hasty," said Bart. "What is it exactly that you want from us, Mr. Cordon? You want something, or we'd all be dead by now."

"Right you are again, Mr. Stanford!" said Cordon in weird excitement. "You are each going to be placed in a position on my staff where you will all be of the most use to both myself and the company. I need to see how well you perform in your given roles before I decide to use Serum #463 on myself…I think, though, for right now, you're all probably just hungry…You're all just hangry. A good meal will perk you right up…"

He reached in front of himself and pressed a button on his desk. There was probably a touch screen on Cordon's desk, but Shane could not see it from the camera angle Cordon was in.

The white door on the right side of the monitor made a loud click, and then it swiveled inward to reveal yet another white room beyond the one they were already in.

"You see…" continued Cordon. "Mmmm…How can I explain this? Let's see…I guess I'll just spell it out for you. Serum #463 was derived from the blood of a rather rare individual currently in my custody. Her blood grants a type of immortality, but that immortality does not come without certain side effects."

Shane's nostrils picked up the scent of something delicious. It was a mix of both a heady and tangy aroma, something that made his stomach growl. He could also hear a sort of thumping sound over and over again in his ears, a strange beat that hit at regular intervals, though that sound was faint.

"Those shutters did not reveal any new kind of laser, Mr. Johnson," continued Cordon. "Those shutters just let in the sun…Just the plain ol' sun you've seen every day of your life…but I'll explain everything after you've eaten…For right now…just enjoy your meal."

Shane was barely listening. He was starving, too hungry to think on any of this at the moment, and that heady, tangy scent was calling to him.

He walked through the open door that led into the next room, and the others followed him.

This new room was a little larger than the one they'd just exited. It was a rectangular white room with short grey carpet, a large flatscreen monitor on the wall to the left of them, and before them was…

There was no food in here that Shane could see. Instead, there was a small group of employees that clearly worked for Cordon, three women and two men, all of them dressed in professional business attire, though they wore bright, conical party hats on their heads.

A woman in her mid-thirties pulled the string on a party popper, the little party favor burst forth its confetti, and the small group all cried out, "Congratulations!"

Shane could smell whatever food was in here; he just simply couldn't see it yet. That thumping in his ears was growing louder, each thump driving him forward to seek that food...That thumping was connected to the food somehow. Oh, yes, he was truly starving, and he could tell everyone else in his little group was as well.

The flatscreen on the wall flipped on as Cordon's irritating and incredibly-punchable face popped up on it yet again.

"One last thing!" said the billionaire in excitement. "To the greeting committee in here! You've all been gathered here today because of a certain...*mmmm*...lacking in your performance...I'm talking theft, extra-marital affairs, sloppy work ethic, etc. That sort of thing makes the company look bad, so thank you for your service, but for one reason or another, I have to let you go. You are all terminated, effective immediately."

The woman with the confetti popper gazed upon Cordon's face with a horrified expression of surprise etched upon her own face, her mouth dropping open in shock.

"Wh...What?" she stammered.

Shane could not control this hunger any longer. His own mouth dropped open as he let out a long gasp of pure shaking desperation. He could smell them, these people, these poor people who had just been fired, and he could hear their heartbeats, that thumping in his ears, and those heartbeats called to him.

But it was little Zuri who acted first. Her lips parted as her mouth opened wide to reveal two large, sharp fangs. She hissed once and then charged on all fours, only to leap upon the poor woman with the party popper. This woman screamed as Zuri's fangs bit deeply into the woman's exposed jugular, and then blood sprayed from the wound to dot the white of the room around them.

The two remaining women screamed while the two men shouted, and that little group tried to run, but their door, the door they had specifically used to enter the "greeting room," would not open for them. There was no handle or knob for which to do so.

The woman that Zuri was attached to staggered around in a circle before falling to the grey carpet beneath them, and Adrian was on that woman a second after that, biting into her left leg, right underneath her grey business skirt.

"Aaahhhgggh!" shouted Bart as he rushed forward.

The old man grappled one of the men from behind, and then he bit into that man's neck just like Zuri, just like Zuri had bitten into the first poor victim's exposed throat.

Donna shrieked and charged, and Quarron charged as well, Donna on the remaining man, Quarron on one of the two remaining women. They attacked from behind, both of them savagely biting into vulnerable jugulars to spray hot red blood around the room.

On some level, Shane felt a modicum of horror, but even he could no longer fight this raging hunger within himself.

He rushed forward out of instinct and pulled back on the blonde hair of the last remaining woman, though this poor young lady had been screaming and pounding on the locked door in front of her.

She cried out in stark terror as he pulled back her head to expose her bare throat, and that fear, that tangible fear that radiated from her like an aura, was an addictive drug that drove his hunger through the roof. His new fangs bit deeply into her jugular, and then he drank in her life essence, his eyes rolling up in the whites as he felt a new surge of power rush through him, a jolt that electrified him right down to his core.

"Don't worry about a thing," said Cordon from the flatscreen. "We'll get all of you set up in the company, and then every one of you will have access to as many real meals as you need. You'll learn security, espionage…assassinations…positions in rival companies, and even political positions, and the best thing about it is, you don't age! So you have all the time in the world to learn new skills…Ah, but for right now…as I said before…just enjoy the meal."

Shane could feel blood dripping down his face as he looked up and over at Donna. She gripped a dying businessman in her arms, her own face coated with the man's blood, but she briefly detached her mouth from his neck and smiled at him, her new fangs red and slick with that liquid life essence.

Shane did not like Cordon, not one bit, but the billionaire was right about one thing…They were all most certainly enjoying their meals.

#3...INTERMISSION

Time for horror in 2nd Person POV!

Your great-great-grandmother only lived to be sixty-three. On her deathbed, she told your great grandmother that she had been cursed by an old woman from the old country, cursed during a "picture show" back when silent films were black and white. This was back during a time when there was a cinema announcer reading off of cards, back when someone played the piano in the background during the film.

Your great-great-grandmother had refused to give up her seat for the old woman, and the old woman had cursed her, uttering something terrible in the old tongue. Your great-great-grandmother was twenty-three at the time, and she had sworn that ever since then, your family has been cursed to never get a good night's sleep. Your great-great-grandmother certainly didn't.

Your great-great-grandmother got pregnant with your great grandmother the very next year. It wasn't until your great grandmother turned twenty-three that she started showing the same symptoms as your great-great-grandmother, that lack of a good night's sleep.

Your great grandmother died at the age of fifty-eight, your grandmother died at the age of fifty-six, and your mother died last year at the age of forty-eight. Your uncle on your mother's side died at the age of forty. In fact, everyone in your family on your mother's side has died too early in life. Their deaths were all the same, all from the same general illness that has plagued the blood of your family ever since that fateful day when your great-great-grandmother refused to give up her seat at the "picture show."

But you don't believe in that curse nonsense. You believe in genetics. Your family members died of natural causes, heart attacks and strokes, and you know those deaths were because of a genetic disorder, that lack of good sleep you seem to have inherited, not some curse.

Even so, ever since you turned twenty-three a month ago, your sleep has been pure crap. You wake up exhausted and shaking, and this isn't doing you any favors for your employment. You need to get some rest just to function, so you want to see a specialist, but you don't have insurance, so that isn't happening.

Thankfully, there's an experiment going on at the local university, a sleep study, so you decided to participate. Because of your unique syndrome, they let you in, even though a ton of people applied for this study.

You've already been paid two-hundred dollars in advance, and you'll get a thousand once all is said and done. They want you to take a new sleep medication, one that's supposed to help you remember your dreams. All you have to do is log your dream in a dream diary after you wake up.

You never remember your dreams, so this should be fun. The university has even promised to look into your individual sleep problem once the study has completed. They find you uniquely fascinating.

You took your first pill an hour before your noon nap, and then you laid down for sleep. You have to go to work tonight, but that's okay. You usually try to catch a few Zs before having to go in, so this is a double boon for you. These pills might even allow you to get some great sleep…You never know.

You wonder what kind of strange dreams you'll actually have, and that thought makes you smile as you close your eyes.

*****

You wake up.

It's night outside of your dingy little studio apartment on the third floor of this building. You can see nothing but black outside of the dirty windows you have yet to clean.

You check your phone. It reads 12:00 AM. You didn't call in to work last night. You know you're in trouble, but hopefully you can talk your way out of this one. Sure, it's only a burger-joint job, but you still need the money. If it weren't for your dad lending you a hand, you'd never even be able to afford this dirty little place.

You flip on the TV. Your flatscreen just has a black screen with the large, white, capital letters "INTERMISSION" printed across it. It's the same for every streaming channel. None of them seem to be working.

You feel like something strange is going on. You groan as you crawl out of your small, twin-sized bed. It's time to put some clothes on anyway, and you want to do a little investigating.

You scrape together some clothes, put on your shoes, and grab the bare necessities: keys, wallet, phone. You catch a glimpse of the TV as you walk to the door. It still states, "INTERMISSION." You shake your head and leave your apartment.

The lights are flickering in the upstairs hallway. There are smears of blood across the dirty beige walls, and you can see bloody handprints here and there. The hairs on the back of your neck stand up as you look around for some psycho, some deranged killer, but you see nothing.

You step back into your apartment, lock the door, and dial 911. You receive a female voice that simply says, "We're sorry, but the number you have dialed is in intermission. Please, hang up and wait for intermission to end."

You hang up.

You go online on your phone. All of the ads that pop up simply read, "INTERMISSION." You go to your favorite news site. You get a 404 error that states, "Page in Intermission." You go to any website you can think of. You get more 404 errors that state, "Page in Intermission." Feeling frustrated, you type in, "intermission definition." The search simply comes up with, "What you are in."

Now you know something is wrong, very wrong.

You head back to the door, unlock it, and open it just a crack. You look out into the hall, but you see nothing but an empty hallway, though the walls are still smeared with blood.

You check the time on your phone. It is 12:00 AM. It was midnight when you woke up. Something is very, very, *very* wrong here.

You carefully enter the hallway, and you quickly use your keys to lock the door. You can always run back here if necessary, but if you do, you certainly don't want a nasty surprise waiting for you.

You creep down the hallway. You need to get to the stairs. There's no way you're taking the elevator in this situation.

You make your way down the hallway toward the stairwell. You hear a door unlock and then the creak of that door opening. You turn to look for the source of the sound, but you see none of the doors you've passed have been unlocked and opened. Your adrenaline spikes as you realize that it's your door that was unlocked and opened.

You stare back at your door in horror as a withered grey hand with sharp black nails appears from out of your doorway. It scrapes its nails along the dirty beige wall right next to your door, leaving trails of white in the painted plaster.

You turn and run for the stairwell. You're definitely not sticking around here.

You open the stairwell door and practically fall down the stairs in your haste. You feel like peeing yourself, but you hold it in. Whatever is going on is thoroughly in a realm outside of your understanding, but you at least know to get out of the building. That's your number one priority right now.

You head down to the first floor and exit the stairwell.

You enter the first-floor hallway. The walls down here are also stained with smears of blood along with bloody handprints. The lights flicker overhead. You need to get out of here.

You exit the building and walk out into the summer heat. It's night out, obviously, but the full moon shines down on the town from above, the moon shining down along with an untold number of twinkling stars. Normally, this would be a great night to take a walk around town, but right now, you're too scared to even think about it. You need to get somewhere safe.

You walk along the sidewalk in the general direction of the police station, at least, where you *think* the police station is. Thankfully, you've never had a reason to head to the police station until now.

Everything is quiet around you as the streetlamps flicker overhead. You hear the opening of the apartment building door, and then that door shuts. You've made your way down the street, so you turn and look, but you see no one around, just empty parked cars with no signs of people or town life at all. You cannot see anyone around your apartment building.

Goosebumps crawl up your arms. You are steadily growing more and more fearful with each step. You can sense something following you. You know it.

You head to the edge of a four-way, but you don't recognize the buildings around you. Unknown shops and a couple of bars are in this old part of town, but the signs on the buildings and windows simply say, "INTERMISSION." You look up at the street sign in front of you, but the green signs on a post simply state that you are on the corner of "INTERMISSION" and "INTERMISSION."

You hear slow but soft footsteps behind you. You turn to look, and you swear you can see a dark, hunched shape move behind a parked car twenty feet from you. You can feel panic rising within you now. You need to get out of here.

You cross the street, instinctively looking both ways for oncoming traffic, but that's stupid in context. The town is dead silent...Not even bugs are chirping.

The unknown shops around you have blood and bloody handprints smeared across the glass of their windows. The parked cars around you are all empty. You can see blood and bloody handprints smeared across those windows and windshields as well.

You pass a black pole with a town clock mounted on top of it. A flickering streetlamp shines down upon the clockface, and you can make out the hands of the clock pointing straight up...It's still midnight.

You do not know what to do. You know something is following you, but you have no idea where to go. You want to panic, but your rational, reasonable self will not allow you to.

You decide to throw a tantrum instead. You walk up to a plastic trashcan outside of a shop and kick it a few times, cussing away as you do. You would have felt better over this little tantrum, but you hear a short chuckle from the direction you came. It sounds like an old woman.

You keep moving.

The hairs on the back of your neck are standing on end. You know you are being followed. You can feel it. It's not your imagination.

You walk down the street and head toward a lit building in the distance. The unknown buildings, bars, and shops around you are all dark inside, but the building ahead has lit windows and a lit door, so you head toward it.

You pull out your phone and call 911 again. You get a female operator's voice that simply states, "We're sorry, but the number you have dialed is in intermission. Please, hang up, and—"

You end the call and swear up a storm. Your mother would have smacked you across the mouth for what you just said, but at this point, you don't care. You need to get out of this crazy place. This can't be your town…It can't be.

You head to the lit building up ahead. You make the mistake of turning around, and in the distance on the sidewalk just twenty feet away, you can see a hunched figure in black robes standing there.

"H…Hello?" you choke out.

The stranger in the distance chuckles. It sounds like that old woman's voice you heard earlier, and it does not sound friendly.

This strange old woman reaches up with her left hand, and that hand is the grey and gnarled hand with the black nails you saw at your apartment door. She runs her nails across the blood-smeared window of a parked car, leaving trails of white behind, trails of scratched glass showcasing the deadliness of those ebony nails.

You stumble as you turn to run, but you catch yourself with one hand before you can fall, your fingertips pushing off the sidewalk in order to right yourself. You run toward the building with the lit door and windows.

You make your way to the glass door of this new building and open that door, scrambling through the entrance to get inside. Much to your horror, you look around and recognize these beige walls…This is *your* apartment building.

The walls of your building are the dirty beige you hate so much. There is still blood smeared everywhere, still bloody handprints on the walls, but now the word "INTERMISSION" is spelled out in large bloody letters here and there.

You know you exited this building and walked across town. There's no way you should have come back to this cursed place. You walked down the street in a straight line. You never got turned around and circled back. You know that. You know that for a fact.

Your brain is frozen in studying this new conundrum, so you do not hear the door open behind you until it's too late. You turn out of surprise, and there is the old woman standing right in front of you.

The top half of her face is hidden by a black hood, but the lower half of her face is a withered, wrinkled, and stark grey. Her black lips are parted slightly, and you can see jet-black teeth lining the red gums of her mouth.

She lets forth a sound that's somewhere between a growl and a shout, a sort of "NYAGH!" sound, and then her left hand slashes at your face with those razor-sharp, ebony nails at the ends of her gnarled grey fingertips.

You instinctively raise your right arm to protect your face. Her nails rake across your right hand, opening up the skin of your palm with ease. You turn and stumble as you catch yourself on the wall, and then you push off that wall in order to run, but not before those deadly nails rake across your back, leaving bloody slits in your shirt.

You leave a bloody handprint on the wall as you run toward the stairwell. There's nowhere to go but up, because you don't think you can get past this thing that attacked you in order to flee back out the building.

You hit the stairwell door and tug on the handle, but the door is stuck. You can't open it for some reason. You pull hard, but the door will not budge…There is no lock on the stairwell door. You know that.

You turn as the old woman in black attacks again. Her nails rake across your left arm as you bring it up to protect your face. Blood wells up from the slashes across your left arm to match the blood dripping from your right palm and across your back.

You kick up with your right foot, but the old hag grabs your leg and slings you around like a toy. You bounce off of the wall on your right and roll across the short, dirty, orange carpet lining this old building. Your fear and adrenaline are off the scale.

You cry out as you are slashed across your legs, back, and buttocks before you can react. You turn over and raise your arms to protect your face, and you are mercilessly slashed across your arms and stomach.

You try to stand up, but you are picked up as gnarled grey hands grab you around the waist. You are tossed into the other wall, spinning in the air as you do, and your breath is temporarily knocked from your lungs as your back impacts that wall. You slide down the wall, leaving a smear of blood behind. You push up off of that wall, but black nails slash you across the left cheek.

She grabs you by your shirt and throws you backwards. You hit the stairwell door and slide down it. You quickly stand up, tug at the handle of the door, and it opens.

You can feel nails rake across your back again as you cross into the stairwell.

You stagger, stumble, and run up the apartment stairs. You are all panic now. You don't know what to do, and your mind is locked in sheer terror. All you can think of is to get back to your apartment and lock the door behind you.

You're bleeding everywhere now, and you're beginning to feel lightheaded. You really need to lay down. You're beginning to feel sleepy.

You make it to the third-floor stairwell door. You open the door and step out into the hallway…

You stop as you take a few steps into the hallway. The door behind you shuts.

The lights are still flickering overhead, the walls are still smeared with blood and bloody handprints, but the word "INTERMISSION" is written in blood all over the walls, over and over again, everywhere, but that's not what roots you in place.

There are bodies everywhere.

You recognize yourself, yourself in different slashed clothes, the bodies of "you" strewn out all across the hallway in different places, in different positions, those bodies slashed and bloody with multiple wounds. There are at least thirty bodies in this hall, all of you…all of *you.*

You stumble forward through this minefield of corpses, this minefield of you.

The door behind you opens, but you're feeling weak. Your mind begins to fog as you try to make it to your apartment door. You turn and raise your arms as black nails slash across both arms at the same time. You turn again, stumble, and catch the wall with your right hand, leaving another bloody smear across it.

You cry out as you are slashed across the back again, and you turn to face your attacker once more. You trip and fall over a body behind you. The back of your head hits the floor, and the sudden blow dazes you.

The old woman standing over you slashes you across your belly. She then picks you up by your waist and pitches you like so much trash. You fly over several bodies, those corpses of you. You crawl in your own blood over one of your own dead bodies.

The pain you are feeling from everywhere is so intense that you can barely move. You are so lightheaded, you can barely think. You know you are going to die, but there is only one thing left on your mind at this moment, only one thing left that you can do.

There is a single clean spot on the wall right in front of you. You reach forward with your bloody right index finger and trace out, "INTERMISSION."

Gnarled grey fingers pull back your head as black nails rake across your stretched, bare throat. A fountain of blood sprays from your gashed throat as darkness closes in around you.

*****

You wake up to your alarm. You groan, reach for your phone, and swipe it to shut down the irritating sound. You pick up the phone and check the time. It reads 2:00 PM. Your nap was two hours long.

You pick yourself up out of bed and wipe the crust from your eyes. The nightmare you just had haunts you, and you don't feel like going to work tonight. You don't even want to write about your nightmare in your dream diary, but you probably will when you start feeling more like yourself.

You dial your boss to tell her you're not coming in tonight, and she's mad at you, but you tell her you'll take Leon's shift tomorrow night. She says she'll call Leon and then call you back.

You get up and grab some coffee. You don't want to go back to sleep. You're afraid to.

Your boss calls you and says that Leon will take your shift today, but he wasn't happy. That's understandable, but you really need a day off to recuperate. You feel like you've been trampled by a rhino.

You sit around and do nothing productive all day. You watch TV, play games on your phone, and surf the net. You don't really feel like existing right now.

You try to write about your nightmare in your dream diary, but the memory of it is too vivid, too fresh…too traumatizing.

You order out. You don't really have the money to waste on fast food, but you spend it anyway. You order pizza. You pay the delivery boy, take your pizza and soda, and lock the door. You're just going to vegetate tonight.

You flip through your list of shows on your TV and decide to watch a romcom. That's the furthest thing you can think of from whatever nightmare it was that you had. You have to get motivated for work tomorrow night, but that doesn't matter right now.

You eat your pizza and watch your show. You get about halfway through it before you get sleepy and your eyes begin to close. Your eyes snap open as you keep yourself from falling asleep. You're still afraid to doze off.

You blink a couple of times as you realize your movie has stopped for some reason. You let out a low whine as you stare at the large white letters on your black TV screen.

Those big block letters simply spell out, "INTERMISSION."

#4...OGRE VERSUS SASQUATCH

The title is not metaphorical.

Irgruuk rose from his kneeling position. He had stepped through the portal the bloodmages had opened for him, and their duty was finished, but now it was time for his to begin.

No metal could be transported through the portal, and in fact, what could be taken through was very little, so all he had was a bearskin loincloth, but that was sufficient. He would find weapons along the way. At the very least, he could craft a rudimentary club out of a fallen tree, and by the looks of where he had ended up, trees were plentiful here.

All around him were the deciduous trees one would see in a temperate climate, a forest teeming with life, something he favored over the harsh mountains and dark caverns his kind normally haunted. He did not know the names of these alien trees, but they looked similar enough to the kinds he was already familiar with that such a comparison did not matter. He was not here for that anyway.

He ran his broad right palm over his bare tanned midriff, his muscles defined to the point where only a fool would challenge him, and that was in spite of being ten feet tall. He was like all other ogres in the fact that he possessed an overbroad chest, a larger-than-normal, bald, round head, and the huge, trunk-thick, muscular arms that could crush stone, but what was not normal was his above-average intelligence, a curse he had been born with, something that had left him dissatisfied with life in general.

A crimson glow emanated from his torso, a bright sanguine hue that shone clearly even in broad daylight. This was where the bloodmages had implanted a waystone, that which would take him back to the Imperium and away from this new and foreign world.

This glow died down and then out altogether after a few seconds, and it would only activate again once he was ready to activate it. That waystone would only glow again once he was ready to return.

But he had a duty to perform first. He was to scout the area, assess threats, assess resources, and then return before any invasion could begin. If this world could not be conquered…no matter. There were an infinite number of worlds out there, though he did not understand the magics behind the bloodmages' scrying that gave the insane elder wizards such knowledge.

Irgruuk moved with purpose now, shaking off the temporary weakness that associated planar jumping. The first thing he was going to do was seek out water, the primary necessity for any length of stay in a new world.

His bare feet stepped over rocks, dirt, sticks, and leaves, the bedding that covered any forest floor, but his thick skin prevented him from feeling any of it, so there was no worry about injuries from exposure. No, he was used to surviving on very little…The Imperium was not a kind master.

He sniffed the air for the scent of water, though catching such a scent would be difficult in a forest rife with woodland smells. Nevertheless, he caught a hint of something, blood and musk, so he followed it. He could smell the faint musk of man in the area, male humans, and mixed with that was the blood of an animal, a fresh kill…He was sure of it.

He took to thumping through the trees on broad bare feet, but it did not take him long to find the source of the scent he pursued. He came across two startled young men kneeling over a felled stag, though these men were definitely of foreign make.

Both young men wore hide clothes of deer skin, that clothing topped by necklaces of fangs and the talons of birds of prey. Their hair was jet black like a starless night, and their skin was ruddy like the color of river mud at the bottom of a dried riverbank.

Irgruuk had never seen such peoples before, not men of this make, but that didn't matter. The only thing that mattered was their weaponry and their prowess with that weaponry, and that was sadly lacking. Their weapons were simple stick bows, bows they immediately armed and readied as Irgruuk advanced upon them and their kill.

He shrugged off their pathetic arrows, the arrowheads nothing more than sharpened stone, not steel, not something that could penetrate his thick flesh. He laughed as the arrows bounced off of him—one, two, three, four—and then he roared out a challenge.

He drew in his breath and then roared out his battlecry, the same vocal challenge that had scattered a division of hardened Morecki soldiers from the Rafspalli Kingdom. He was Irgruuk the Destroyer, though the two young fools in front of him did not know that, but they soon would.

And they did.

The two young men abandoned their kill and ran, leaving the felled stag, a definite boon for Irgruuk to consume.

He did not follow them. No, he was going to eat this stag, scout a little further, stay here for the duration of his allotted month, and then report back to the Imperium. If all there was to this world were opponents such as these, the Imperium would soon rule here.

Still, he needed to find water. He had food now, so that was good, but finding water was going to be a little more difficult…unless it rained. Rainwater would do just as well.

Irgruuk recovered a primitive stone knife one of these primitive young men had left behind in his primitive haste. Now Irgruuk also had a tool with which to cut, albeit a tiny one in his huge hands.

It occurred to him that he would do well to follow the hasty tracks of the fleeing natives. Where they had fled to had to lead to water, so he picked up the stone knife, tucked it into his bearskin loincloth, and then slung the dead stag over his left shoulder.

He smiled to himself, his face splitting wide to reveal his large, broad, flat teeth. He had not been here for even an hour, and already he was ahead of the curve. This was his first time scouting an entirely new world, and he was clearly a natural for it…The Imperium would be pleased.

He followed the tracks of the young men—the turn of twigs here, the step marks in dirt, the torn leaves—and it was not long before he came upon a babbling brook that flowed from northwest to southeast. He could tell the directions due to the position of the foreign sun in the sky, as it had been moving in the same way and timely fashion his own world's sun moved.

He dropped his newly-won stag, knelt, and cupped his broad hands within the stream before him. He drank deeply of fresh clean water, something in rather short supply within the desert region his masters had moved him to. No, the Imperium had stationed him within the Morecki Desert on the Rafspalli border, and that was where he would return once he had finished his duty here, here in this strange and primitive land.

He decided this place was as good as any to set up camp. The sun here was lowering in the west, so night was going to fall, and he wanted to get some food and rest before continuing on in the morning. This was his first day here, but he was allowed to laze around for one night. He was afforded some freedoms.

The bloodmages could see him; he was certain of that. They were scrying on him right now, scrying through a pool of blood, seeing through his eyes, but once again…he was afforded some freedoms.

He *was*, of course, on a deadline…He had to return by the end of a month, or the waystone inside him would automatically take him back. Naturally, others had tried to defy the Imperium, but trying to remove the waystone would detonate it…Once a slave of the Imperium, always a slave of the Imperium.

He took to the task of skinning his prized meal as he thought briefly upon his past.

They had found him when he was but an adolescent, a young brug wandering the Dragon's Tooth mountainside within the Wyrm's Teeth Range, and he had killed five of their trappers before they could put him in chains. He had been transported to Degrasjao after that, and it was there that he had grown up with masters and inferiors. It was there that he had learned to be a full-grown orug with a purpose, unlike his wretched kin…They were still wandering that mountainside.

Irgruuk had started out his new life in Degrasjao in the arena. He had plenty of scars to prove that, but he had also become a champion there, and from there he had moved to the Imperial Army, and now he was here. This was his reward.

He ate his stag raw without cooking it, for his kind was used to eating as such. Nevertheless, he would need to find some way to make fire at some point, preferably sooner than later. As an adult ogre, he had some protection against the cold, but that did not mean he liked a descending chill, and he did not know how cold it would get here in the evenings. Besides, he liked the taste of cooked food anyway. He had grown accustomed to it.

He finished his meal and laid back upon forest earth with his hands behind his round, bald, broad head. Tomorrow was a new day, and with new days brought new dangers and rewards.

He would seek out the village that owned the young hunters he had chased off, and then he would subjugate that village. The Imperium would be pleased at such a promising start, and Irgruuk would be further rewarded.

He thought back upon the feasts he had partaken in, the human female slaves he had mated with, and the times when he had been praised by his masters…These were all fond memories. He would have new accolades and benefits upon his return; it was inevitable now. This world was his for the time being, and the bloodmages would get an eyeful while he was here…He was definitely going to give them one.

He smiled his broad smile as he closed his eyes. The sun was setting behind the trees, and he was going to sleep until dawn, something of a treasure for a slave of the Imperium.

*****

Irgruuk's eyes snapped open as he awoke to the sound of loud knocking. He held his breath and waited, listening, and then he heard it again, a loud knock of wood on wood, as if someone were striking trees in the distance.

He heard a loud calling after that, a hooting of sorts, but not from any bird. The calling raised and lowered in pitch to form grunts, and then the knocking began again, a knocking of wood on wood, like one tree striking another.

He raised himself up on both palms as he struggled to see through the black of night. He did not know how long it would be until sunrise, but he did not really need light in order to see what he was dealing with.

He heard the calling again, and then he smelled it, the intruder or whatever it was. His sense of smell recoiled at the merest touch of the odor, something so foul he could not quite describe it. It smelled like rotting flesh mixed with decaying food mixed with stinking feces…Horrific.

He rose to a standing position and peered around his immediate area, but other than the sounds of the babbling brook mere feet away, he could not sense anything else. He could not sense where this loud and very-smelly intruder was.

He let his eyes adjust to the darkness around him. His kind were used to dark caves, crags, hollows, and underground caverns, so the pitch of night around him was not insurmountable.

He could see the outlines of trees now, and he listened, listening for the unknown that had wandered into his territory.

He saw it before it could strike him, a blot of black arcing toward him, and he stepped aside as a large stone thunked into forest earth on his immediate left. He knew the direction from which it had sailed, so he opened his broad mouth and roared out a challenge in that direction. Whoever had thrown this stone was a fool, because now they had angered him, and now they were an enemy, and enemies would be crushed.

Another stone came sailing toward him, but he stepped aside to avoid it, just as he had the first one.

Enough was enough. Irgruuk bent his knees, hunched his broad muscular shoulders, and then took to running. It was time to charge.

He charged into the dense foliage that sheltered whatever had thrown the stones. He was going to catch this interloper, grab them with both hands, and then snap them in half.

He was ambushed from his peripheral left.

Irgruuk saw the swinging tree just in time to grab it, but the force of the swing actually pushed him in a semicircle as his left side absorbed the blow. The strength of it was surprising, true, but he had fought mountain trolls, so he was used to facing things possessing such power.

But the smell was ungodly. Whatever it was that clutched the other end of this felled tree? It stank to the highest heavens.

He could see it now, and it was big. It was at least eight-feet-tall, a couple feet shorter than him, and it was slenderer than him, but it was definitely humanoid, probably some type of giant like himself. It was covered in dark fur or hair, and its face had the rough semblance of a man, but he had never encountered anything that looked even remotely like it.

Irgruuk knew what was going on now. Those two boys had run back to their village and had told the story of their encounter with him. The humans' elders had probably summoned this foul-smelling thing in response to Irgruuk's invasion…

This thing's stench proved its otherworldly presence. It was some type of demon, or perhaps a guardian spirit of the forest, but it was not undefeatable. Once he sent this hairy giant back to the hell it had been summoned from, he would deal with the human village and its elder mages. Their magics were primitive compared to his masters' arts, so he had nothing to worry about there.

Irgruuk's feet stopped sliding across the forest earth, and he pushed back against the hairy giant wielding this thick tree trunk like a club. This smelly thing took a few steps backwards, and then it pushed back. It roared as he roared in return, and then the tree the both of them clutched snapped in half, splinters of wood flying here and there from the savagery of their colossal struggle.

It did not waste time in its reprisal.

The hairy giant swung its half of the tree above its head, swinging it in an arc toward Irgruuk's own head. Irgruuk blocked the blow with his own half of the tree trunk, the wood knocking against wood, but he felt the impact of that mighty blow, that impact sliding his huge bare feet backwards.

Irgruuk swung his own tree trunk at his smelly foe's left knee, but this hairy thing expertly blocked the blow with its own tree-half. They beat upon each other's tree logs for a few strikes after that, and Irgruuk could tell that this forest guardian had experience with this type of combat…but this was getting nowhere, so Irgruuk detached from his opponent's range, backpedaling in order to charge forward yet again.

He charged and then swung his crude weapon toward the thing's left midriff, right where its ribs would be. This creature swung its own club at Irgruuk's left side at the same time, and both tree clubs impacted at the same time, both tree-halves striking unprotected flesh in unison.

Its strike was a little higher than Irgruuk's, but that didn't matter. What mattered was Irgruuk's ribs breaking on his left side, the bones cracking with microfractures as he did the same to his enemy. Both of them staggered to their respective rights from the opposing force and the sudden pain, but this only lasted for a second…The real battle had just begun.

The hairy creature dropped its tree-half as Irgruuk dropped his. They were on each other after that, both engaged in a grappler's clutch, Irgruuk's massive hands on this smelly thing's shoulders, its hairy hands upon Irgruuk's muscular shoulders. They danced in a circle as they both struggled for superiority, and Irgruuk had to admit that this horrendously odiferous guardian of the forest was just as strong as he was.

Irgruuk took to striking it in the face with his right fist as it did the same to him. They struck each other with thunderous blows six times in fashion before this new type of punishment grew old.

Irgruuk roared as it roared right back at him, and then it bit into his left arm with a savage, bestial rage.

The pain was intense, but it was nothing he couldn't handle. He cried out as he pulled back on the hair on its head to successfully pop its mouth from his left arm. The wound on his lower left arm was dark with blood in the pitch night, and that sparked something inside him, something that pushed him over the edge.

This enraged him, the sheer ferocity and audacity of this thing, and Irgruuk snapped. He wrapped his thick arms around its hairy waist and then picked it up, charging as he did. He slammed the creature to the forest floor and mounted its hairy stomach, bringing down his fists as he did, raining blow after blow upon its hairy face.

Unfortunately, this enraged the creature beneath him. It reached up with its right hand and clutched the back of his head, and then it forced Irgruuk's face to the dirt through sheer raw power. It struggled out from beneath him after that, struggling out only to stand above him.

Irgruuk felt himself being lifted, being *picked up*, for the first time in his life. He was lifted into the air as this hairy beast raised him up above its head on two incredibly powerful arms. Irgruuk was slammed to the forest floor after that, planted into the dirt like a flung toy from an angry child.

His breath left his lungs. This had never happened to him before, so he was left unprepared as the smelly wild beast mounted his stomach and began raining blows down upon him now.

It was learning from him.

Irgruuk drew in his breath and did his best to block shots with his left arm as his right arm flailed in the dirt, his massive right hand searching for something, anything to get this thing off of him. His thick fingers touched hard stone, and he clutched a large rock in his hand after that.

It would do.

He brought up the stone and shattered it across the hairy beast's thick skull. The creature pitched to its own right, Irgruuk's left, and this gave Irgruuk enough time to stand and recover his wits. The creature was up from the dirt in nothing flat, so what time Irgruuk did have to recover his wits was very little indeed.

It charged him this time, and Irgruuk was lifted up as it wrapped its hairy arms around his muscular waist. He was picked up and charged forward after that, only to be slammed down into the babbling brook he had camped next to. He was slammed down into the water, and then one terribly-powerful right arm held down his face beneath the flowing stream.

This thing was trying to drown him, but Irgruuk was still the superior grappler. For one thing, he had no body hair.

He reached up with his right hand, gripped a good portion of hair, and pulled this thing's head to its own left. The creature's weight shifted enough to where Irgruuk slipped out from beneath it.

He stood to face it, but it was fast, faster than he had originally estimated.

The creature roared as it reached down between Irgruuk's legs, reaching beneath his bearskin loincloth…reaching for his genitals.

It was playing dirty now.

Irgruuk made the wise decision to back up and away from it, and the two squared off once more.

If only he had his hammer, he'd have killed this creature by now, but he did not have it. He did not have his huge war hammer and his protective chainmail, so he would have to take it out hand-to-hand, and that was proving to be no easy task.

This thing was ferocious, true, it was powerful, true, and it was learning from him, true, but he was still its superior. He was Irgruuk the Destroyer, he was a force to be reckoned with, and he was going to deal with this guardian of the forest, this force of nature, and then he would punish the village that had summoned it upon him. He would tear their elder mages limb from limb.

They both charged at the same time, both clashing together, their big feet stomping around in the babbling brook beneath them.

Irgruuk clutched his huge hands around its neck as it wrapped its hairy palms around his own. Neither one of them had much of a neck, or rather, their necks were thick reinforced trunks that could withstand a hurricane.

They spun in a circle, both squeezing, both wheezing from the sheer pounds of pressure put upon each other's throats.

It had tried to play dirty before, so now it was time for Irgruuk to play dirty.

He brought up his right leg and kneed it squarely between its legs, but he didn't stop there. He kicked again in immediate succession and planted his big bare foot in this thing's solar plexus.

The beast popped off of him as it sailed backwards to land upon its back outside of the confines of the brook. Irgruuk was on it after that, ready to show off his superior skill, because he had been fighting this fight all the wrong way, and he knew that now. This creature was intelligent, true, but it was wild and untrained, so it was time to use that inexperience against it.

He quickly flipped the beast over to its stomach and mounted it, mounting the small of its hairy back, clutching its chin with both massive hands. Irgruuk leaned back after that, ready to end the beast from this position. They both roared as ungodly strength was pitted against ungodly strength, but this did not last long, not this time.

Irgruuk strained with all of his terrible might. The creature's back bent until there was a loud "CRACK!," and then Irgruuk turned its head until there came the satisfying follow-up "CRACK!."

He released his grip after that, and it dropped dead to the forest floor.

He stood up, gave one loud bellow of victory, and then limped away from the dead and terribly-smelly beast.

But he was actually injured now.

Irgruuk had suffered injuries before, true, but never to the point where he had trouble fighting. He'd taken on trolls before, but he'd had weapons and fire, so they had not proven too difficult for him to take down.

His face was swollen from multiple blows, he had a savage wound on his left arm, broken ribs, an injured right leg, a wrenched neck…Still, he would do his duty and hit the primitive village tomorrow. He needed to establish dominance right away, or these elder mages would summon another one of these things, although such summons were costly and involved human sacrifice. Even so, he could not allow such a summoning to happen again.

He went back to the skeleton of the stag he had eaten and fished up his stone knife from out of the bones…It was time to move on from this area. He would not be caught unawares again.

It was a good thing he had eaten right after getting to this new world, because he was going to need that energy to heal. All he really needed was time, just a little time to…

There was a loud "THUNK!" as a large stone hit the forest floor next to him. He looked up to see them, all of them, at least twelve of the creatures now, the terrible and foul-smelling beasts all surrounding him in a circle.

He understood now.

Those humans hadn't summoned the beast that had attacked him. No, these things were the true masters of this world, and the primitive humans that did live here were *allowed* to live here with these creatures' permission…No, the Imperium would not be taking this world. They would not be able to gain a foothold here as long as these things existed…That was a certainty.

If only he had his hammer…

The circle closed in on him.

He did not have time to do the ritual of return. Only his masters could pull him back without performing the ritual, and they typically did not tolerate failure.

He was going to die, but if he were going to die, he was going to go out with a literal bang. He plunged his stone knife into his belly, using his great strength to pierce his thick skin, ignoring the searing pain that followed. The waystone in his belly glowed a bright sanguine hue in response to his fingers digging into his own flesh in order to remove it.

He felt the heat before he felt anything else. The sanguine light around him grew as a glowing crimson portal enveloped him. His body was pulled from this new world, wrenched out of time and space as his masters demanded his immediate and abrupt return. On the one hand, he felt some pride that he was too valuable to lose, but on the other hand, he felt that old anger of knowing he was enslaved.

He was suddenly jealous of these foul-smelling creatures that ruled this new world. They were wild and free, unsullied and untouched by the ruling hand of powerful masters. They were their own masters, and they would be still after Irgruuk was long gone from this accursed forest.

If it was one thing he understood, he understood his own situation…Once a slave of the Imperium, always a slave of the Imperium.

#5...SHOWDOWN

The sins of the father are visited upon the son.

"Why don't you help Mr. Oldfield unload the wagon, Johnny," said Mr. Cartwell.

"Yes, Mr. Cartwell," said Johnny.

Mr. Cartwell ran Cartwell's General Store, and the job Johnny had here was boring most of the time, but Johnny's ma wanted him to have a proper upbringing, and with no pa to speak of, he was stuck here for the time being, here in the small town of White Cross.

Johnny was thirteen, but he'd be fourteen soon, and he was already taller than his ma. He had a shock of sandy-blonde hair on his head to bely his own thoroughly tanned skin, skin darkened by many days of work in the hot sun, and today he was in his white cotton work shirt with his brown trousers and brown suspenders, good brown leather work boots on his feet.

This was the style and look he almost always dressed in, and since his ma had no complaints with that type of dress, he'd never really felt the need to change it.

His ma was a widow, because his pa had died back when he was only seven, but his pa's death had taught him some things about life in general, and he kept those lessons close to his heart at all times.

His ma was fortunate enough to work for Mr. Cartwell, and that was why Johnny worked for Mr. Cartwell too, though he only got a third-pay. That was nowhere near what he wanted, what he deserved, but he'd get that soon enough. He was determined to put his pa's history in the past where it belonged, start a new life, and be someone respectable that would make his ma proud.

But he still had a job to do in the here and now.

Johnny walked outside to tend to Mr. Oldfield's wagon. There were bags of flour, bolts of cloth, little goods like spools of thread and wooden boxes of needles, and other such sundries waiting to be unloaded from the wagon. Mr. Oldfield was inside the store collecting his payment from Mr. Cartwell, so it was up to Johnny to get things started.

"A good morning to you, Johnny Tucker," came a familiar voice.

Johnny turned to eyeball Lillian Magner. She was his age, but she had been paying him a lot more attention as of late. Her pa was rich and owned the bank; the man had made his fortune after the war.

He really didn't understand Lillian, though. A rich girl like her didn't need to be bothering a poor widow's son like Johnny. Her visits irritated him a little, especially when she used his full name.

"Do you always gotta say my last name?" frowned Johnny.

The young lady sported a fine sky-blue dress with white flower embroidery, and in her white-gloved hands was an equally fine white parasol. Her blonde hair was done up in curled braids, a new style of coif she was probably showing off, probably to him, though he didn't care for that sort of thing.

She twirled the parasol around in her fingers and shone him a clever smile.

"It's a sign of respect, Johnny," she said wistfully. "You could do with a little class."

"I been to class," said Johnny. "Ma says I gotta go."

He hopped into the back of the wagon and picked up a couple of large bags of flour.

"Not that kind of…Never mind," sighed Lillian. "Anyway, I can see you're hard at work today."

"Yep," nodded Johnny. "Mr. Cartwell needs me to unload these goods for the store. Mr. Oldfield will unload too as soon as he comes to an agreement on payment with Mr. Cartwell. I hope they hurry up, too. It's gonna be hot today. That sun ain't showing a mercy to me."

"I've heard that Mr. Cartwell is going to give a certain someone the store once he passes on," said Lillian. "It's on account that he has no children."

"Oh?" asked Johnny. "Who's that?"

Lillian rolled her eyes, and Johnny immediately figured out who that "certain someone" happened to be.

"Naw," he replied in firm denial. "That ain't right. Cain't be me. Where'd you hear that gossip?"

"I overheard Mrs. Pritcher telling Mrs. Olsen," nodded Lillian. "I was down at the bank with my father."

"Yeah, yeah," waved off Johnny. "My ma would a said something to me if that were true. Even if it is, I don't want to run no general store."

"What's wrong with running the store?" asked the young lady in audible confusion. "My father says that's a good and upstanding job."

Johnny continued to unload goods from Mr. Oldfield's wagon, but this conversation was starting to grate on him. Nevertheless, Lillian hadn't particularly said anything mean to him, so there was no reason why he couldn't explain himself.

He picked up a large sack of flour and moved it underneath the awning at the back of the store. He'd move the goods inside after he was done unloading the wagon.

"If you really want to know…" said Johnny. "If you really want to know, I'm gonna be famous. I'm gonna be a gunslinger like my dad."

"Johnny, your father was an outlaw," said Lillian. "He was hanged."

"Yep," said Johnny.

He acknowledged that fact, and he had figured she would say that anyway.

"That don't mean I have to be an outlaw," he continued. "I'm gonna be a deputy first, and then I'll move up to sheriff. Then, I'll head to Texas to be a Texas Ranger."

"Oh…" said Lillian, but she did not sound happy.

He studied her pretty face for a moment, but she looked just as unhappy as she had sounded.

"What?" he asked.

He was unsure as to why she would be unhappy about his life choices, but their conversation was interrupted by a newcomer, a voice Johnny had never heard before.

"Those who live by the sword die by the sword," came that unfamiliar voice.

Johnny turned to address this new stranger.

A tall and thin man stood before them, this stranger dressed in the black cloak and white collar of a preacher, though he had a wide-brimmed black-felt boater hat over his narrow face to keep off the heat of the sun. He had a hard face, one used to wind and rain, so he was a traveler, though Johnny had never seen his like before, not here in White Cross.

"Then said Jesus unto him," continued the stranger, "put again thy sword into his place: for all they that take the sword shall perish with the sword. The Gospel of Matthew, Chapter Twenty-Six, Verse Fifty-Two."

"The chapel's that way, Mister," nodded Johnny. "I take it you're here to see Preacher Goodie?"

"Ah, yes," nodded the man.

Johnny studied him, but for the life of him, he could not tell this man's age. This man had clearly lived a hard life, so he was anywhere between thirty and fifty…Johnny simply couldn't narrow down a range of years.

Johnny felt Lillian's hands around his waist. The young lady was holding onto him, hiding behind him in fact, her head poking around his right shoulder, though why she would be afraid of a preacher-man, Johnny had no idea.

"Are you replacing Preacher Goodie?" asked Johnny.

"No," said the tall stranger. "No, I'm just passing through. However, I shall stop at the White Cross Chapel and speak with Preacher Goodie."

"Who are you, Mister?" asked Johnny.

“I am Missionary Malach,” nodded the man. “You must be young Johnathon Tucker. That means the young lady behind you can only be the lovely Lillian Magner.”

“You have me at a disadvantage, Mr. Malach,” frowned Johnny. “How is it you know our names?”

The tall stranger smiled, though his smile was not comforting in the least.

“White Cross is a small town,” he said. “Your names are not unknown to me.”

“Right,” nodded Johnny. “Well, it was a pleasure meeting you, Preacher Mala—”

“*Missionary* Malach,” corrected the tall man.

“Right,” nodded Johnny again. “Missionary Malach. It was a pleasure meeting you, but I gotta get back to work. These goods don’t move themselves.”

“Of course,” nodded the missionary in return.

He started to leave in the general direction of the chapel, but he stopped, turned, and gave Johnny one last cold smile.

“Remember this well, young Mr. Tucker,” said the stranger. “Beware the darkness in your own heart. Those who seek darkness shall find it.”

Now Johnny did not like this. He did not like strangers up in his business, especially some preacher-man with a high-and-mighty attitude.

Johnny answered the man with a short tone, though he had not intended to be short with him. This man had simply rubbed him the wrong way.

“I’m counting on it, Mister,” frowned Johnny.

“Are you now?” asked the missionary. “You should not say such things, young man…Therefore all things whatsoever ye would that men should do to you, do ye even so to them: for this is the law and the prophets. The Gospel of Matthew, Chapter Seven, Verse Twelve…We treat others with equal kindness, compassion, and mercy, Mr. Tucker.”

“I’ll treat a no-good varmint like they deserve, Mister,” growled Johnny. “That ain’t nothing a bullet cain’t cure.”

“So be it,” grunted the stranger. “You will learn one way or another, Mr. Tucker, though I doubt you will enjoy the lesson.”

The tall man dressed in black walked off after that, not even turning his head to look around. No, he made a beeline for the chapel in the distance, but Johnny was fine with that.

"Good riddance," muttered Johnny.

"You shouldn't be rude to a pastor, Johnny," said Lillian quietly.

Johnny turned and gave her an incredulous stare.

"You're hidin' behind me, and you're gonna give me a lecture on rudeness?" he asked in disbelief.

"He was kind of scary," shrugged Lillian. "He might be right, though…"

"Oh, really?" asked Johnny.

He was feeling uppity now.

"And what might he be right about?" he asked.

"Maybe you shouldn't be a lawman," said Lillian. "Working at the store is a good way to make a living…and…you might get shot and killed being a deputy or…or a sheriff."

"Nah," he said as he waved her off. "I ain't worried 'bout that. I been practicing with my pa's old pistol…I'm fast. I learned my pa's tricks. Only good thing he done for me…Yep, I can outdraw any no-good outlaw. Just you wait. I'll have my name in the papers."

"Can you even shoot?" asked Lillian.

"Of course, I can shoot," frowned Johnny. "I can hit a bullseye at ten paces, no fooling. I carry my pa's pistol with me to work and back home. Practice with it every day. I can even wear his old gun belt. Mr. Cartwell makes me put it away in the store, but it's in there. He gives me a discount on bullets, though he don't like the idea of it. He don't want me to end up like my pa, but that ain't gonna happen. I'm gonna be a deputy as soon as I age a few, so…yep, I can shoot."

Lillian stared down at the dry ground as her face darkened with what looked like worry. Johnny shook his head at the expression, for he did not know what to make of it.

"What?" he asked.

Lillian shook her head and refused to speak for a moment.

Johnny shook his own head and walked back to the wagon out of both necessity and frustration. He still had a job to do.

He hopped up into the wagon and dragged out three bolts of cloth. He moved those three bolts of cloth beneath the awning at the back of the store and then turned to address Lillian again.

"Johnny, I…" began Lillian, but her sentence trailed off as it ended with a gasp.

Alarmed, Johnny turned to study the frightened expression upon her pretty face.

"What?" he asked. "What is it?"

"Johnny…" said Lillian, her lips aghast. "You…You don't have a shadow!"

"What?" asked Johnny. "What are you…"

He looked behind himself to view the brightly-lit ground where his shadow would be. The sun was beating down upon the both of them, and in fact, that celestial orb was beating down upon the entire town of White Cross, yet he had no shadow.

Johnny turned, walked ten paces, swiveled around, and then walked back again. No matter which direction he turned, he still had no shadow.

He felt a cold spell sink into him, a chill that traveled straight down to his bones. Something mighty strange was going on here, but what that could be, he had no idea.

"Maybe we should take you to Preacher Goodie," said Lillian in a hushed tone.

"No," said Johnny in emphatic denial. "Whatever's going on, it'll fix itself. I ain't going to the preacher, not unless things get really bad, but that ain't gonna happen. Everything'll be fine by tomorrow, you'll see."

"I hope so…" said Lillian, but she sounded unsure.

Johnny certainly hoped so, too. He didn't like the sound of this, but he felt physically fine, so…he really hoped everything would right itself.

*****

The sun was going down in the west.

Johnny was currently taking inventory of the day's stock as Mr. Cartwell counted the money he had made off of the day's business.

The interior of the store was stuffy and hot due to the summer heat, but Johnny was used to it. Things would cool off once the sun went down anyway.

He turned and gave a brief glance toward Mr. Cartwell. The shop owner looked up at him from behind the store counter and nodded once in return.

"You'd better get on home, Johnny," said Mr. Cartwell.

"I don't live that far away, Mr. Cartwell," said Johnny.

"I know, but your ma is waiting for you, and no one likes to eat supper in the dark," said the man. "Summer days are long, but the time can slip away from you. I do appreciate the extra help you put in, though, Johnny. You're a hard worker."

"Thank you, Mr. Cartwell," nodded Johnny.

"Why don't you skedaddle," said Mr. Cartwell. "You can come in late tomorrow, okay?"

"If that's what you want," said Johnny.

"You've earned it," said Mr. Cartwell.

"Okay, then, Mr. Cart—" began Johnny, but he was cut short.

The door to the general store opened as Samuel Magner walked in with Lillian. Johnny had not expected to see either one of them in the store at this hour, and apparently, neither had Mr. Cartwell.

"Why, Mr. Magner!" said Mr. Cartwell in excitement. "I hadn't expected you in here!"

"The store is still open, is it not?" asked the wealthiest man in town.

Lillian's father was a dapper man sporting a fine brown suit, a waxed handlebar mustache, and a nice brown bowler hat. He carried a brown wooden cane in his gloved left hand, though Johnny seriously doubted the man needed it to properly walk.

"Of course, of course!" nodded Mr. Cartwell. "Come right on in!"

"Excellent," said Mr. Magner in return.

"What can I do for you this evening?" asked Mr. Cartwell.

"It's more what you can do for my Lillian," said Mr. Magner. "She was wondering if that Parisian parfum had arrived today."

"Yes, yes," said Mr. Cartwell. "That's a rather expensive item, but it arrived, nonetheless."

The shopkeep turned and reached up for one of the small box-shelves on the wall behind the counter where the smaller, more-expensive items were kept.

"I have it *riiiiiiight* here," he drawled out.

He pulled out the crystal bottle of overpriced liquid and took to wrapping it in brown paper.

Mr. Magner took that moment to walk up to Johnny and look him over.

Johnny did not understand what all of the eyeballing was for, but he suffered it for Lillian's sake. He did not want to embarrass her in front of her own father.

"You must be Mr. Tucker," said the dapper man with a slight frown.

"Yes, sir," nodded Johnny.

"Well, straighten up, young man," said Mr. Magner. "Don't slouch…Let me have a look at you…I've heard good things about you. I've heard you're a hard worker."

Johnny straightened up as best he could and then answered as best he could.

"Yes, sir," he said firmly. "I ain't…I haven't missed a day since I started working here."

"Hmm…" said Mr. Magner with a brisk nod. "Well…keep up the good work. White Cross needs more people with integrity."

"Yes, sir," said Johnny firmly. "I will, sir."

"Well, I must settle my debt with Mr. Cartwell," said Mr. Magner. "Good day, Mr. Tucker."

"Pleasure meeting you, sir," nodded Johnny.

The dapper man parted Johnny's presence and quickly settled his debt with Mr. Cartwell.

"You should take a lantern with you, Mr. Magner," said the shopkeep.

"Our driver has lanterns on the carriage, Mr. Cartwell," said Mr. Magner. "We'll be fine."

"Then good evening to you, Mr. Magner," smiled Mr. Cartwell. "Don't be a stranger now."

"Of course," nodded the wealthy man.

Johnny nodded at Lillian as the pair took their leave. The young lady smiled in return, a strange expression of contentment upon her pretty face. Johnny did not know what was going on in her head, but whatever he had done or said, he knew he had impressed her.

"It's time for you to get a move on too, Johnny," said Mr. Cartwell. "Mr. Magner may not need a lantern, but you should grab one just in case. You don't want to run into coyotes in the dark."

"I'll get the old lantern, but I got my pa's gun, Mr. Cartwell," said Johnny. "I ain't afraid of no coyotes."

"Well, you be careful with that pistol, youngin'," warned Mr. Cartwell.

"Yes, sir," sighed Johnny. "I been practicin' every—"

He did not get to finish his line of verbal thought. The loud bang of a gunshot echoed outside right along with the accompanying sound of shattering glass.

Johnny hit the floor for cover as Mr. Cartwell ducked behind the counter of the general store.

"Get down, Johnny!" yelled the middle-aged man.

"You're preachin' to the choir," said Johnny in a hushed breath.

He looked up to see that one of the corner windows of the store had been shot out. It occurred to him in stark reality that Lillian was still outside, as he seriously doubted her carriage had left yet. This panicked him in a way he had not foreseen, and he reacted as such.

"Lillian's out there!" he yelled. "I've gotta go get her! I need my pistol!"

"Johnny, keep down!" barked Mr. Cartwell. "Let the law handle it!"

But Johnny was already on his feet and running into the back stores to grab his pa's pistol. His pa's old Colt Dragoon was a trusty piece that Johnny was well practiced with, and now he was getting the chance to use it.

Johnny strapped on his gun belt, even as more shots rang out in the night. The sun had completely set, so whatever was going on outside was made even deadlier by the fact that there wasn't anything out there but lantern light. There was lantern light in the store, of course, but that was of no help right now.

"Johnny, don't be a fool!" yelled Mr. Cartwell. "You'll get yourself killed!"

"Sorry, Mr. Cartwell!" yelled back Johnny. "I gotta save Lillian!"

He opened the front door of the store, ran out onto the wooden deck, and immediately ducked behind two of Mr. Cartwell's empty shop barrels.

He could see Mr. Magner's carriage, as it was lit by four lanterns hanging down from its four corners. The four horses drawing the carriage were chomping at the bit, the driver crouched down in a huddled position beside those horses, desperately attempting to keep them from bolting.

Upon further inspection of the scene, Johnny could see Mr. Magner lying in the dirt of Main right next to his carriage, Lillian crouched above him.

"Lillian!" he called out.

Against his better judgement, he ran out to the pair, though he knew this was a truly stupid thing to do.

Lillian looked up at him with fearful eyes.

"Father's hurt!" she cried.

The wealthy man sat up and clutched his left arm above the elbow.

"It appears I've just been grazed," he said unhappily. "The cowardly cad ran off after firing several rounds at us."

"Did you get a look at him, Mr. Magner?" asked Johnny.

"No," said the injured man. "He was a tall man in black, but he was cloaked in shadow, so I don't know who he was."

The town was already ablaze with more lanterns, and the sheriff and his deputies had arrived, guns out and ready. Johnny was certainly glad for the sight of them.

"The law'll get 'im, Mr. Magner," nodded Johnny.

"I know they will, young man," frowned Mr. Magner. "I'll make sure of it."

*****

Johnny stood outside the front of Cartwell's General Store, broom in hand, ready to sweep. He had just taken to the task when he looked up to see Lillian Magner, though this time the young woman was dressed in a white dress with red roses embroidered upon it. She was lovely as always, though Johnny didn't think on such things often.

She twirled a large white parasol between her fingers and gave Johnny a once-over.

"Johnny Tucker," she smiled.

"Lillian," he said in return.

He took to sweeping again, mindful of her presence, but he would let her start the conversation. He wasn't much for talking with girls anyway.

"I was worried about you," said Lillian.

"Worried about me?" asked Johnny in disbelief. "What in the heck for?"

"You still have no shadow, Johnny," frowned Lillian. "I can tell, even though you're standing under the awning."

"I…" started Johnny.

He shook his head and continued sweeping. He was not going to think about that.

"I ain't worried about that," he said unhappily. "That'll fix itself; I'm sure of it…Let's talk about something else. What are you here for anyway?"

The young woman frowned in return at Johnny's curtness, but then she sighed and changed subjects anyway.

"I wanted to thank you for coming to our aid," said the young woman.

"Eh, it's okay," shrugged Johnny. "Somebody shot at your pa. It's been the talk of the town this morning…Don't you worry, though. I'm sure the law'll get that no-good varmint that shot at ya. They'll fill him full a lead. Just you wait…Heck, I was ready to put some bullets in him, myself. Cain't believe someone would shoot at you, Lillian. Makes no sense. If somebody did shoot you, I'd put him down like a dog."

"Johnny, I—" began Lillian, but she did not get to finish her sentence.

"It's a difficult thing to kill a man, Mr. Tucker," came a familiar voice.

Johnny looked up to see the tall and dark stranger from the day before, this "Missionary Malach." The man had appeared like a ghost in the street, like some specter that had made its unwanted presence known.

Malach was dressed in his black missionary garb, a wide-brimmed black-felt boater hat on his head, his look finished by fine black boots on his narrow feet. His dark outfit made his sudden appearance feel even more uncanny than it should have been.

Whatever the case, Johnny did not feel like taking any guff from this strange preacher.

"Is that so?" asked Johnny in open defiance. "I reckon you just aim and pull the trigger, mister."

This gaunt man, this "Missionary Malach," leaned his head slightly to one side and gave Johnny a stern and discerning look.

"It's more than just pulling the trigger, Mr. Tucker," said the clergyman. "It's the consequences that come with it."

"The consequences for shootin' down a criminal?" asked Johnny in disbelief. "That's what the law is for, Mr. Malach!"

"The law is for keeping the peace, young man," said Missionary Malach. "It is not for killing with impunity."

"You're saying the sheriff and his deputies cain't defend themselves?" asked Johnny.

"It means they must abide by their duty," said Malach. "They may be forced to kill as a last resort. However, they are not judge, jury, and executioner."

"The law's my hero, mister," said Johnny through narrowed eyes. "If it weren't for them—"

"Heroes save lives, Mr. Tucker," said Malach. "They don't take them."

"Says you," argued Johnny. "I'm gonna be a Texas Ranger when I get older, and I'm gonna hunt down varmints like that one that shot up the town last night."

"Texas Rangers bring in wanted criminals for judgement," warned the missionary. "They only kill when they are forced to."

"I know what the Texas Rangers are like," frowned Johnny. "I don't need you to tell me that…I ain't my pa. I ain't gonna be like him. I'm gonna hunt down criminals."

"Will you now?" asked Missionary Malach.

The tall and slender man in black held a grim smile on his face.

"I know all about your father, young man," he said. "Your father fell in with Robert Peach."

Lillian gasped, and Johnny took a brief second to look over at her surprised face. He'd known who his father had run with, but that didn't mean the whole town had to know.

He looked back at the missionary, ready to give the busybody a piece of his mind, but Mr. Malach spoke first, and what he said stopped Johnny from completing any sentence.

"That pistol of yours wasn't even your father's," said Malach.

He nodded toward Johnny's right, and Johnny looked over to see his pa's gun belt and pistol on top of the empty store barrels, the same store barrels he'd hidden behind just the night before.

"Wait…That's back in the storeroom…" said Johnny in confusion.

He snatched up the belt and quickly inspected it, but one thorough glance told him that it was indeed his pa's.

"*That* is Robert Peach's Colt Dragoon," said Missionary Malach. "He killed over thirty men with that gun. He gave it to your father as a reward for helping him rob the bank in Veldt, sixty miles from here."

"How do you know that, mister?" asked Johnny.

Something was wrong here, very wrong. Even Johnny hadn't known that about his pa.

Johnny quickly strapped on his pa's gun belt, even as the preacher-man continued on with his diatribe.

"I know many things that you do not, Mr. Tucker," continued the tall man in black. "However, that is not the issue here, nor is it relevant to my umbrage with your position…No, my teaching is thusly so…There is nothing wrong with being a lawman. What's wrong is your disregard for the lives of others, and that is the legacy disgraced upon you by your father."

Johnny locked his gun belt in place. Whatever was going on, he needed to be ready, especially with Lillian out here.

"My pa was no saint," scowled Johnny, "but he was still my pa, and you don't badmouth someone's pa, mister. Preacher-man or not, you best git before I fill you full of lead from Robert Peach's Colt Dragoon."

"You should have learned your lesson last night," smirked the strange and hostile missionary. "I thought you had learned something by seeing to the safety of others, but it appears another lesson is in order."

And that's when it clicked. Johnny knew what was going on now, and he was furious.

"*You* shot at Mr. Magner!" he cried. "It was you!"

"Me?" asked Missionary Malach. "The darkness in your heart is out roaming free, young man. No, you need to point the finger at yourself, *young Mr. Tucker*. Better yet, why don't you look to the sky."

Johnny stepped forward off the porch to confront this hostile clergyman, but he stopped cold as the sky began to darken.

He looked up to see the black round of the moon slowly crawl across the sun, something he'd heard of in class, something called an "eclipse," but he'd never thought he'd live to see one.

"What is happening, Johnny!" cried out Lillian.

"What is this, mis…ter…" began Johnny, but his voice trailed off as he realized something very important.

The strange missionary was nowhere to be found.

Johnny turned his head left and right, but there was no sign, no trace of the hostile clergyman.

People from around White Cross left their buildings and houses to view the strange, once-in-a-lifetime event.

The sky grew as dark as night as Johnny kept his right hand over his pa's gun.

He walked slightly down Main and then moved in a trot toward the sheriff and his deputies. He was going to report that missionary posthaste.

He had just walked up to the lawmen when shots rang out in the street. The very people he looked up to dropped around him as Johnny ducked down and searched for somewhere to run. Sheriff Williams fell first, then Deputy Smith, and then Deputy Adams was shot down right after that, one, two, three in an ambush of bullets.

Johnny's mind, however, ditched the idea of protecting himself. No, his thoughts shifted toward Lillian, and he backed away from the fallen lawmen as he turned to address her safety.

The young woman had walked out into Main like all of the other townsfolk, probably on a hesitant path to follow Johnny, though she had left her parasol behind on the porch-deck of the general store. Nevertheless, her curiosity had now put her in danger, and that was something Johnny could not help but panic over, because now she was frozen with fear; he could tell that even through the descending darkness.

"Run, Lillian!" yelled Johnny.

The young woman took off toward the entrance of the store, but she never made it there. Dirt kicked up in a cloud as bullets impacted right in front of her, effectively freezing her advance. Lillian shrieked as she fell backwards to her rump, but she was uninjured; Johnny could tell that from a quick glance.

Johnny turned in a circle to see where the gunfire was coming from.

There was just enough light from the eclipse for Johnny to see the assailant of White Cross. A shadowy figure stood at the end of Main, but it was not the tall and slender form of Missionary Malach. No, this new man was all dark, wreathed all in shadow, all except for a pair of red eyes, red eyes that pinpointed Johnny's position in the dirt street, homing in directly upon him.

"Boy…" said the man from down the street.

This attacker was some distance away, but for some reason, Johnny could hear him just fine, even over the screaming and the slamming of doors around Main.

The stranger wreathed in shadow holstered his piece and gave Johnny the staredown, a staredown consisting of two piercing red eyes, two terrible scarlet-orange eyes that burned a hole right through Johnny's soul.

Johnny's right hand shook as it hovered over his pa's gun.

"Who are you!" yelled Johnny.

"That's my gun…" said the man in a guttural voice, a voice that sounded graveled over with swallowed sand.

"R…Robert Peach?" stammered Johnny.

"Robert Peach gave me that gun…" said the man. "Now…draw, boy…"

It hit Johnny right then, a revelation of insane proportions, and he did not like the implications of it.

"P…Pa?" stammered Johnny yet again.

"Draw, boy…" said the hostile stranger.

"Y…You cain't be my pa," said Johnny in disbelief. "My pa's dead…"

"Draw, boy…" repeated the gunman. "Draw…so I can take back my gun…"

Johnny felt his knees buckle. Now that he was in a tight situation, a situation he'd often daydreamed about, a showdown, he did not want to be in it. He did not want to be in this fight, certainly not against his own pa.

"I cain't…" said Johnny in vocal obstinance. "I cain't do it. I…I…I cain't fight you, Pa."

"Draw…" commanded the shadowy man. "Draw…or I'll kill the girl."

Lillian whined as Johnny gave her a quick glance. He looked back toward the stranger and shook his head no.

"You…You cain't kill people no more, Pa," he said in a wavering voice. "It's wrong!...Why would you wanna kill Lillian anyway? She ain't done nothing to nobody!...You…You gotta turn yourself in, Pa."

The man grunted out a short, guttural laugh.

"You're not my son…" said the shadow man. "You're just a lily-livered coward…You've got no gumption, boy…I brought you into this world…and now I'm gonna take you out of it…I won't have no coward for a son…You've got no right to wear my gun…I'm taking it back, boy…but first, I'm gonna kill that pig-banker's daughter…and then…I'm gonna kill you…"

"P…Pa…" choked out Johnny.

He did not want to cry, but he felt that unwanted moisture stream from his eyes anyway. He did not want to be here, not here, not like this, but he did not have a choice.

"Time's up, boy…" said the shadowy figure. "Die like the coward you are…"

The clock on the bank's arch struck noon, and the chapel bell rang out in time.

The hostile man wreathed in shadow drew on Lillian, and a shot rang out in the dark, but Lillian did not feel any pain from that shot, nor would she.

The shadow man staggered back a few steps before falling to his back.

Johnny's eyes were wide and wild as he stared down at the smoking gun in his right hand. He had outdrawn his first adversary, outdrawn his own pa, and he had done it without thinking.

Light streamed down from the sky as the eclipse ended. It was subtle at first, a sliver of gold that shone past the passing moon, and then the sun was back to its blazing glory shortly thereafter.

The people of White Cross walked out of their buildings and homes to enter Main. They went about their business, ignorant or uncaring of the events that had just unfolded.

Johnny stared in openmouthed shock as the sheriff and his two deputies stood and walked on as if nothing had happened to them, as if they had not just been brutally murdered in the street.

He looked to the body of his pa, but the shadowy figure from the dark was gone, no trace of him, not even a speck of blood.

"Put that gun away, Johnny!" hissed Lillian.

Johnny quickly holstered his piece as the young lady dragged him away from the center of Main, dragging him toward the only place he currently needed to be, and that place was on the front porch of Cartwell's General Store.

He did not know what had just happened, but he did know that things appeared to be normal again, and that was all that mattered. The first thing on his mind, however, was concern for the safety of Lillian.

He unstrapped his gun belt and set it aside as he addressed her. He needed to know if she was all right.

"Are you okay?" he asked her.

"Are you okay?" asked Lillian in return.

"I…I don't know…" he stammered.

He really didn't understand what had happened or what was going on, but he felt like maybe he had dreamed it all, a nightmare, but the young woman next to him confirmed the reality of what had just happened.

"What happened, Johnny?" asked the young lady. "Everyone is just going about their business like nothing happened. Even Sheriff Williams and the deputies are walking around like they weren't even shot. I don't understand."

"I don't either," breathed out Johnny.

It hadn't been his imagination. Lillian had seen it all. Lillian had seen everything that had happened. He wasn't a madman after all.

He wiped his face clear of tears and shook his head in resolve. It wouldn't do for a man to cry in front of a woman. He had a new goal in life anyway, a more positive one, one that didn't involve killing…No, he'd lost his taste for killing…It did not suit him well, but that was nothing to cry about. He figured that to be a good thing. Besides, he had someone who was special to him in his life, though he had not realized that fact until just now.

"I know one thing," he said in a shaky voice.

"What's that?" asked Lillian.

"I don't wanna be a deputy anymore," said Johnny. "At least, not right now."

"What?" asked Lillian.

"I think I'll just work in the store for a while," he replied. "I'm not sure I'm cut out for the law, but I'll think on it…Besides, I…I want to be around just in case you need me. I cain't do that if I'm off yonder wherever."

"Oh…" said Lillian in surprise, but then that surprise turned into a wide smile upon her pretty face.

"That's a good attitude to have, Mr. Tucker," came the stern voice of Missionary Malach.

Johnny swallowed a gulp of saliva as he turned to look upon the tall and imposing clergyman. The man stood in the dirt of Main, his dark eyes locked upon Johnny and Lillian, but the expression upon his gaunt face was not so grim anymore.

Johnny's first reaction was to stand in front of Lillian.

"What do you want, mister?" he asked warily.

"Nothing, Mr. Tucker," smiled the dark missionary. "It appears there is nothing more for me to teach you. You've conquered your darkness and fixed it to your feet where it firmly belongs."

"I don't know if that's a compliment or not," frowned Johnny.

"It's admiration," smiled the tall and dark man.

He nodded toward Johnny's shoes, and Johnny turned to look down toward his own two feet to see what the man was talking about, but he solved that mystery the moment he laid eyes upon it.

"Johnny, your shadow came back!" gasped Lillian in excitement.

"Well, I'll be…" said Johnny, but he did not have time to think on this strange occurrence.

Johnny turned back to address Mr. Malach, but a group of young ladies passed by the missionary as the man in black stepped back to let them through.

Johnny recognized Mary O'Conner, Elizabeth Glenhouse, Belva Moore, and Dahlia Turnkey.

The tall redhead of the group, Mary, turned, smiled, and waved at Johnny.

"Hello, Johnny!" she said as the whole group of four walked up to him.

"Hello, Mary," nodded Johnny.

The group of young ladies giggled as they walked past both Johnny and Lillian and entered the general store.

He turned to see the deep and unforgiving scowl upon Lillian's face directly after that, but he did not understand why she would be so out of sorts.

"Is somethin' wrong?" he asked.

"It does not do well to wear your jealousy like a bonnet, young lady," said Missionary Malach.

Lillian gave him a loud "Humph!" and shook her head no.

"I'm not jealous of some blacksmith's daughter," said the young lady. "Besides, she has her father's ungainly hands and feet. Why would I be jealous of that?"

"We treat others with respect," frowned the dark missionary. "For someone who speaks of respect, you do not show it."

"I don't have to respect her," scowled Lillian. "She's never shown any to me."

"That is irrelevant," said Malach as he shook his head no. "We treat others with respect, even if they do not show us the same in return. That is the path of the righteous. Furthermore, we trust in those we love because trust is the foundation of our love for one another."

Johnny didn't quite understand what was going on here, but he was pretty sure he wanted no part of it. Riling up Lillian was a bad idea anyway.

"Uh, mister—" began Johnny, but he did not get to finish his warning.

"I am *not* jealous of Mary O'Conner," spat Lillian. "But, *I might add*, there is nothing trustworthy about her. She's nothing but a low-class peasant who talks above her station. She's just as crude and as shifty as her father…No, I don't trust that family at all. In fact, I think my father needs to have another look at the debt Mr. O'Connor owes him."

Now, this was getting out of hand.

"Uh, Lillian—" began Johnny again.

"Your prejudice and envy are as plain as the nose on your face, young lady," frowned Missionary Malach. "You should study the Parable of the Unforgiving Servant. You need to learn a lesson in humility."

"*You* need to learn to mind your own business," warned Lillian. "And if you don't, I'm sure Sheriff Williams can show you to the edge of town. You can conduct your business there."

The tall and gaunt man in black simply tipped his wide-brimmed black-felt boater hat and put forth a grim smile, but Johnny didn't like that look at all.

"So be it," said Missionary Malach in a firm tone. "Good day, Ms. Magner. Mr. Tucker."

They watched him walk off after that, his path headed toward the White Cross chapel.

"Good riddance," spat Lillian.

But Johnny didn't like the idea of arguing with the strange missionary. He knew that man was more than what he appeared to be.

"Lillian, maybe we should just…" he started to say, but his voice trailed off as he noticed something very important.

"What?" asked Lillian, a slight irritation in her voice. "Why do you look so disturbed, Johnny Tucker?"

"Lillian…" said Johnny as he sucked in his breath. "You ain't got no shadow!"

#6...PARKING LOT

It's the Ides of November.

"**That'll be** sixty-one thirty-three," said the young woman behind the counter.

This young lady was the type of new-age pop junkie that Barbara couldn't stand, a vapid record-ghoul with little aspirations outside of whatever new single hit number one on the charts. Nevertheless, Barbara suffered the young woman's presence out of necessity rather than the alternative, and the alternative meant leaving without the clothes she had just wasted an hour on, a whole hour gone for just a few shirts and skirts.

Time was money, and that saying was more popular than ever in this modern business world, but spending both time and money were far easier than saving them.

Decisions, decisions. Barbara sighed and made hers, though she knew she was going to regret it later.

Barbara handed the clerk her credit card, and the young lady ran it through her card checker. The young clerk handed back the card a second later, the store receipt printed out, and Barbara was handed that slip of paper to sign.

Barbara scrawled out her signature, handed the clerk the store receipt, and then took her copy.

"Thank you, and come again!" smiled the young lady behind the counter.

Barbara left the store without saying a word, her plastic bag of new clothes hanging from her left arm, her brown-leather purse hanging from her right. Both containers were unwieldy, though her purse was arguably the much heavier of the two. The bag of clothes was simply a nuisance to carry.

She walked past a line of open stores, her heels clicking upon the multicolored mall tiles. It was getting late, and the mall would be closing in an hour…It was time to go home.

She stopped in front of a newspaper dispenser in order to adjust herself. She set down her bag and purse, made sure the brass buttons of her burgundy wool coat were properly buttoned, adjusted her burgundy knit beret, and brushed a strand of fiery red hair from her left eye. Maintenance of one's appearance was a key to success, especially if that person was a woman in this modern business-centric world.

She knelt slightly to pick up her bag and purse, but the headline of the newspapers in the dispenser caught her eye. Curious, she opened her purse, dug out her wallet, unlatched it, and took out a quarter. She put back her wallet, set down her purse, and fed the newspaper dispenser its sacrificial change. She opened the blue metal box and removed a single daily edition for her own perusal.

The headline read in bold black letters:

PARKING LOT KILLER STILL AT LARGE

She shuddered at the thought of such a monster wandering around the streets. In her opinion, the world didn't need *real* monsters…The human kind were bad enough.

Barbara shook her head clear of any waxing philosophy and continued to read:

November 22nd, 1986

Lyndon E. Rince, Corgan Times Reporter

Magdalene Dagwell, mother of two, was found slain just outside of her own vehicle last month on October 22nd, her body discovered by night-security watchmen, Oliver Gordon and Jamal Diggs, at the Maxington-Wells Shopping District in Corgan Eastside. The 34-year-old woman had suffered multiple stab wounds to the chest and abdomen, over twenty, according to the coroner and local police. This makes the fourth victim in four months, all four victims women of varying ages.

The first victim, Jennifer Rosenstock, age 24, was discovered murdered in the Thompson Theater parking lot, North Corgan, on July 22nd, the second victim, Marion Cresson, age 48, was found slain in the South Love Lounge parking lot, South Corgan, on August 22nd, and the third victim, Gillian Goldstein, age 29, was found murdered in the Ol' Raider's Grocery Store parking lot, North Corgan, on September 22nd.

All four victims suffered multiple stab wounds to the chest and abdomen. No personal items were taken from the scene of each crime, including money. The victims were simply stabbed and either died at the scene or were discovered but died before help could arrive.

Police Commissioner Brandon Dubois made an emergency statement on all local channels last night, that statement concerning the recent deaths of these four victims:

"What we have here in Corgan is something we had only previously guessed at, and that is a serial murderer. As of a week ago, we have agents from the Federal Bureau of Investigation here to oversee the capture of this animal, but for the time being, the citizens of Corgan are advised to stay inside tomorrow night.

"I know Saturday night is the night to go out on the town, and I understand that, but if you must go out tomorrow night, please travel in groups of at least three. Right now, we don't have enough evidence to know what we are dealing with, so stay indoors, travel in groups, and call our tips line to report any suspicious individuals.

"So far, the M.O. of this serial murderer is to attack women who are traveling alone. The four victims were attacked while walking to their cars in the parking lots of various locations. This killer has struck at night on the 22nd of each month, and we fear the attacker will strike again tomorrow night."

Local media and law enforcement have dubbed this new serial murderer, "The Parking Lot Killer."

A terrible chill sank into Barbara as she stared in semi-panic at the print upon the paper. It would be just her luck to be out alone on the night in question, and this did not sit well with her…It left a sucking pit in her stomach.

She picked up her bag and purse, stuffed the barely touched newspaper into a nearby trashcan, and headed for the mall's north exit.

She made her way to the glass doors, only to stare momentarily into the darkness lurking outside…She had parked in the small, out-of-the-way lot.

Her car was out there, her little, grey, two-year-old Ford Escort, out there in the night in the most out-of-the-way lot of the mall. That lot was small compared to the other lots, but it was by no means *small*. She was going to have to walk to the end of that lot, and…

She hesitated to push open the glass.

Maybe she could just hole up here, and…

No, that was stupid. The mall was closing soon.

"This is stupid, Barb," she whispered to herself. "Get a grip. You're stronger than this."

She closed her green eyes, took in a deep breath, released it, opened her eyes, and pushed open the glass.

"Here goes," she said to herself.

She stepped out into lamplight, fluorescence shining down on her from little, round, glass circles overhead, those lights embedded in the flat brown plasterwork of the mall entrance and exit arch above her.

She did not make it five feet before she realized someone was standing in the archway corner off to her right.

There was a young man standing there, a young man in his early twenties, a real greaser-type, this young man smoking a cigarette in the shadow of that corner. He had on a white tank top, a sleeveless blue jean jacket, and a red bandanna underneath his mussed brown hair. His blue jeans had seen better days, as they were ripped in the knees, though his white sneakers looked fairly new.

He noticed her wayward stare and nodded once at her, blowing out a trail of smoke before saying anything at all.

"Hey, sweet cheeks," he grunted. "Why don't you bend over and give me a quickie?"

Barbara's adrenaline spiked as she sped up her walk, her heels clicking on pavement as she crossed the mall threshold into the parking lot. There was no going back now, not with that thug standing there.

"I gotta sausage you can wrap those sweet lips around, Red," said the young man. "All four of those sweet lips, baby."

She heard him chuckle once as she made her way out into the dimly-lit night. No, there was no going back now.

She briefly turned her head to see the young man flick away his cigarette. He plunged his hands into his pockets and stepped forward as if to follow her, and this immediately spiked her blood like nothing else.

Barbara turned her vision forward out of panic. She let out a slight whine of fear as she sped up her walk and made her way into the rows of cars before her, careful not to take a tumble in her heels, though such a balancing act was always trying.

She ducked behind a small red hatchback in order to catch her wits and her breath. It was cold out here, and her breath filtered out in visible bursts of steam, pulling at her lungs, making her already lengthy journey even more difficult.

She hid for a few seconds before raising up to see where the young punk had gone.

The bright lights of a police cruiser pulled up in front of the mall, and she breathed out a visible sigh of relief as two police officers exited their vehicle in order to confront the young man. They would see to it that this thug got what he deserved.

She continued her journey across the lot after that, though her car was at the far end. It was still quite a walk in the cold, quite a walk past the stoic lines of empty parked cars, but the police were patrolling the area, so there was nothing to be afraid of now.

Her heels clicked across pavement as she made distance between herself and the entrance of the mall. There were tall street lamps strategically placed in rows along the lot, so visibility was not an issue, but the vibe that soft light gave, the liminality of it, creeped into her and settled there like so much rot.

She first saw him out of the corner of her eye, a wisp of shadow, a brief passage of something dark a couple of car lines over. She stopped walking and stared in that direction, and that's when she saw the outline of a black fedora, a shadowy figure congealing into shape after that, a dark figure blending into a dark background behind a tall red truck.

Barbara sucked in the chill November air as she took to walking again, this time at a faster pace, her heels clicking out a staccato beat as she stumbled and had to catch herself on an old Mustang.

She stared out into the distance. She could see his outline there, this dark stranger, the outline of a fedora, maybe a suit, but he was in the dark, outside of the protective rings of light from the tall street lamps of this godforsaken parking lot.

A chill wind blew, and a sudden noise ambushed her from behind. Barbara turned with wide eyes to witness an empty pop can roll across the greyed asphalt. The empty can rattled along as it tumbled underneath a town car, disappearing from her vision altogether a second later.

She clutched her chest, clutching her burgundy wool coat from the sudden scare, and she sucked in cold air as she tried to steady herself.

"You're seeing things, Barb," she thought unhappily. *"Keep it together."*

She took a couple of seconds to grip her wits before pulling those pieces back together again. Panicking was not doing her any favors.

"It's fine," she muttered. "Everything's fine…"

Barbara felt the hairs raise on the back of her neck, on her arms, and even on her legs, the goosebumps quilting over with tremulous, tangible fear. She slowly turned around to see him standing there in her open lane, standing between the two rows of cars like she was, though he was five cars down.

He was not quite within the lamplight. No, he was in the dark rim between the soft circles of luminescence that spelled out safety.

This man was tall, a little over six feet, but she could not make out any features save for his broad shoulders, the rough outlines of a business suit, and his fedora. He was so cloaked in darkness that he looked like living shadow, but this was not what spiked her adrenaline to new heights. It was the black outline of a long, sharp knife in his right hand that did that.

"*N…Noooo…*" whined Barbara.

She took to running without thought or heed of consequence.

Her right heel turned as she took a tumble on grey asphalt. She felt her wrists and knees absorb the shock of that fall, that pain nearly insufferable at any other moment, but she was too wired on her own internal juices to give that discomfort much thought.

Her heavy brown leather purse hit the pavement and jangled from the contents packed within it, but she had no time to consider the safety of anything within that carryall. She had to make tracks as fast as she could, make it to her car or to anyone who could help her, because she was not going down without fighting to her last breath.

She ripped off her heels and pinched the foot holes between the fingers of her right hand as she was up and off again, this time without any unbalancing footwear. The pavement was unforgiving upon her feet, as the only thing protecting her bare soles was a thin layer of pantyhose, but she ignored the jabbing bites of small pebbles and debris in order to run for her life.

She rounded a blue Ford pickup and turned to look for her attacker. The man was swift and silent in his own right as his shadowy presence appeared off to her left, between a town car and a compact.

Her green eyes darted from left to right and back again as a reactionary plan formed in her mind.

Barbara flattened herself on the pavement, laying down as best she could, and then she shimmied underneath a nearby small white truck of foreign make. She held in her breath as she lay perfectly still beneath that truck, clutching her belongings close to her like makeshift armor, including her burgundy knit beret; she did not want to lose her favorite hat.

It was not long before she felt a cold seep into her, seeping in past the protective layers of her wool coat. Her green eyes widened as her body trembled at the sight of the dark shoes and suit pants that walked in silent steps next to her hiding place, silent steps that walked slowly but with definitive, murderous purpose.

She could see his outline now, but he was…unnatural. He was just a shape, just a shape of living shadow, wisps or tendrils of black floating up from the pit of darkness that made up the outline of his shoes.

She could sense the evil radiating from this man, for he was not a man, he was something else, something wholly indifferent to the descriptions put forth by rational men, something not of this world.

His presence was like a cancer, like a swallowing void that sucked in a soul in order to crush that soul in its singularity. Barbara had never experienced anything like this presence before, this unholy, defiling entity that walked in silent, murderous steps, but she was not stupid, so she held in her breath, held it in until it felt as if her lungs would burst.

The shadowy entity moved on, eventually walking past the vehicle and onwards towards somewhere else.

Barbara shimmied out from underneath the foreign truck after waiting for a couple of minutes, carefully placing her hat back upon her head. She had her bag of new skirts and shirts, she had her heavy brown leather purse, she had her beige heels in her right hand, she had her burgundy knit beret, and most importantly, she had her life.

She sucked in cold air as she replenished her breath, adding to what was left in her lungs. It had felt like an eternity underneath that truck, but if she were careful—

She turned and saw the dark edge of a shadowy blade streak toward her face, but her adrenaline was still spiked, her senses wired, so she stepped back just in time, a hair's breadth of space between the tip of that blade and her own ruby lips.

She could feel the absolute chill of that weapon as it left behind crystalized air in its wake, cutting a deadly swath through cold air to leave behind even colder air…She had no desire whatsoever to feel that icy sting.

Barbara took to running yet again. An idea possessed her, a half-formed, half-baked idea that made sense to a child or a panicking individual, and she was most certainly the latter. She had to get out of this parking lot, because maybe this thing was like a headless horseman; it had rules it had to follow. Maybe this shadowy wraith could only haunt parking lots, so it made sense to her to head for the nearest edge, to bolt like mad for the border of this parking lot, to run out into the nearest street.

Pebbles and debris dug into the pantyhose covering her soles as she ran between cars, running for her life, but then she saw it, sanctuary, a ring of light, a tall street lamp in this parking lot with a single car beneath it, a single silver Mercedes-Benz parked within that lamp's comforting glow.

She headed for that car at top speed…well…as fast as her bruised and shredded feet could take her.

It had occurred to her that the edge of this lot was too far away, but light, pure and shining light, could protect her from this otherworldly *thing*, and the street lamp ahead either used a stronger bulb or had a short in it, because it was blazing in comparison to any of the other lamps in this hellscape of grey pavement and parked cars.

Barbara could see a woman now, a woman in her early thirties or so, close to Barbara's own age, in fact. This woman was in the process of setting down several bags as she fished for her keys out of her off-white purse.

"Help me!" screeched Barbara as she made a beeline for this stranger.

Startled, the woman stared in confusion and a little fear as Barbara ran up to her.

Barbara got a good look at this stranger as soon as she closed the distance between them.

This woman was a dyed blonde in a brown fur coat, though her coat was open, unbuttoned to reveal a slinky white dress with a low top and a high skirt. This blonde was clearly out shopping with someone else's money, brazen in her tawdriness, showing off her goods in spite of the cold November chill that permeated the atmosphere of this cursed lot.

God, this woman was the kind of woman Barbara despised, the trophy-wife, gold-digging, lawyer-latching head louse that attached herself to men for money and goods…but she was also the only help in the area, so other options were not…well…an option.

"Excuse me?" asked the stranger, verbal surprise evident in her voice.

"I need help!" cried Barbara. "There's a man after me! He's the Parking Lot Killer!"

"The what?" asked the woman.

Barbara could tell that this woman had no idea of the danger the city was in, of what had been going on recently.

"Haven't you seen the news!" exclaimed Barbara. "The Parking Lot Killer! He's here!"

"What are you talking about?" asked the blonde. "Wait…The Parking Lot Killer? Is this about those murdered women?"

"Yes, yes," nodded Barbara in a crazed up and down head wag of visible agreement. "He's here! He…He chased me…He's not humaaa…uhhh…"

She was going to omit that last part. She needed this woman's help, but saying that a wraith from the deepest pits of hell was after her? She would not get any help that way.

"We need to get to a police officer," said Barbara with a gulp of saliva. "Please, give me a ride across the lot. I saw a police cruiser earlier…"

"I didn't see anyone on my way to the car," said the woman in audible confusion. "This lot's pretty empty. I think people will be leaving the mall soon, though…"

"He's here; I'm telling you!" cried Barbara.

She was sounding hysterical, true, but they were running out of—

The fine hairs on the back of her neck stood on end again. She turned out of a survival instinct, and that's when she saw him yet again, his shadowy form lurking between two cars in the distance, outside of this circle of light.

"Th…Th…There he is…" stammered Barbara in a shaking treble.

The dark entity walked forward with murderous intent, the black shadow blade in his right hand a line of infinite void that radiated doom. Barbara could see the chill air crystalizing around this *thing* that vaguely resembled a man, this *thing* from outside the reaches of sanity.

"Where?" asked the blonde in more confusion.

The shadow man marched forward on steady, silent feet. Barbara sucked in the cold air around her as her green eyes opened wide with terror. She was frozen from her own fear now, trembling in place, her own voice ending in a whine to pull forth one last gasp of warning.

"He's *right there*!" she squeaked out.

"There's nothing there…" was all the blonde could say.

Barbara could do nothing but shake as the shadow man stepped into the light and embraced her. She felt his cold left hand wrap around the small of her back, his pitch lips kiss with chill purse against hers, and the absolute-zero essence of his blade sink into the pit of her stomach. She lost herself again as his dark presence enveloped her, overwhelming her.

Her green eyes rolled up in the whites as she felt that old familiar call consume her psyche, a call she could not resist, a call that hit her approximately once a month anymore.

Her back was to the thirty-something blonde behind her, and that was good, because it was time to prepare for the next stage of this eventful night of dark joy.

Barbara smiled as she opened her heavy brown leather purse, heavy due to its jangling contents, and she pulled forth one of those items, pulling forth one of the many knives she had stuffed within that leather container.

She let it glint in the lamplight for a moment.

"I don't see anything," said the blonde. "Are you sure you're okay?...Maybe you should wait here while I go get—"

Barbara turned and plunged the knife into the belly of the pristine white dress this woman was wearing, feeling unbridled joy as the victim's red lips gasped open in shock, feeling the warmth of blood, this trashy blonde's lifeforce, spill over her right hand, the ecstasy of it exciting her, electrifying her in the lowest of places.

Yes…the first stab was always the sweetest.

#7...PUMPKIN EATER

The secret ingredient is love.

Peter looked over the plain and broad wooden table within his kitchen. The pie-crust dough had been made fresh and had already been carefully laid in the tins, so everything was ready for baking.

There would be many guests today, yes, many guests. They would all be waiting for a portion of his delicious beef pies spiced with cloves, the crust mixed with pumpkin. It was his grandmother's recipe, a recipe as old as Methuselah, and he was determined to follow it to the letter…especially today.

This was all for Dora, of course. Oh, she was the love of his life, the apple of his eye, married for thirteen years now, and not a moment wasted. They were so happy together. Yes, *happy*…That was the word.

She was beautiful, with short golden hair trimmed in the fashion that was so popular today. She had ocean-blue eyes, a ruby smile, perfect teeth, perfect skin, and a slender body. Oh, the nights they'd had over the many years! She was a winner, yes, she was.

Of course, it hadn't all been roses. Dora was…difficult…to put up with at times. She had a razor tongue, as sharp as any knife, and she knew just where to stick that blade to inflict the most pain, twisting and twisting and twisting…

Still, he loved her. She was so beautiful, so wonderful, so amazing…

And then there was Margie. Margie was Dora's best friend, or maybe her best frenemy…It was hard to tell. Margie was really…well…untrustworthy. She'd already cheated on her husband, and Peter didn't need any gossip to know this was true. After all, he was the one who had slept with her…multiple times…but she had that effect on men. She somehow always got what she wanted, and if she wanted a man, she took him.

Margie could control a man with only her silver words and her silken body language…Peter had fallen into her arms a number of times now. It was his insecurity with Dora that did that to him, his low self-esteem with the woman he loved that drove him into the arms of the seductress.

It wasn't like he hated Margie…He'd just had enough of her.

He'd never tell *her* that, of course. She was far too dangerous to cross. There was something about her that raised a red flag…something in her dark and mysterious eyes that cornered him and made him cower.

Nevertheless, Margie had always been there when Dora had denied him his nightly advances. Margie had long curly black hair, a beautiful face, a luscious, nubile body, big squeezable breasts, a big squeezable butt…Everything about her was squeezable, though she was far from overweight. She was a sexual hourglass, just the perfect choice to relieve his undeniable tensions.

That, and she had been the one to inform him that Dora was cheating on him with Margie's own husband…Peter had seen the pictures. He had seen the act. He had heard the things they had told each other, had seen the things they had done to each other…but Margie's husband was a lawyer, so it wasn't like Peter could have gone after him…not in the legal sense anyway.

It was one thing for Peter to cheat on Dora, but it was entirely another for her to cheat on him, especially with a lower-than-slime scumbag like Margie's husband. It sounded like hypocrisy, but it really wasn't. Peter was still entirely devoted to his own beautiful wife, not Margie, not the dark seductress that led him around by the nose like he was some kind of…some kind of slave.

No, Margie still couldn't compare to Dora…No, Margie had nothing on Dora. Margie would have to become Dora in order to compare to Dora, and the day that she did, then and only then would he love her, love the wicked seductress that whispered dark thoughts in the back of his mind.

Of course, it would not do to have Dora wandering into the arms of another man, but Peter had a solution for that little problem, a solution that would solve that problem forever.

He clapped his hands together in excitement, and snow drops of flour puffed gaily above the tins…Today was the day, and oh, what a day!...But…

He had a sudden breakthrough, a flashfire of memory that flamed into existence without warning. It attacked him without mercy, and he clutched the sides of his broad head as he suffered through it.

No! He didn't love Dora! He did not love that terrible woman! He wanted out!…He'd wanted out for years now…He wanted to…He wanted…The singing in his head…The children…They were…They…

He could hear the children singing in the recesses of his psyche, skipping rope to that old nursery rhyme he loved so dearly:

"Peter, Peter, pumpkin eater…"

No, this was his day, it was, it was. This was his day for Dora. She was all he needed. This was the day, it was indeed. Now everything would be perfect. The guests would arrive soon. Dora's whole family and his whole family were coming, including their aunts, uncles, nieces, nephews, and of course, good old Mom and Dad.

He whistled a jaunty tune as he slid out a large butcher knife from its protective wooden block. He stared wistfully at the razor sheen of the blade. He could see Margie's face in the reflection of that blade, not his own, not like it should have been, his reflection, his face, his block of a face with a bushy black beard.

Margie was smiling at him in that reflection, smiling and…and whispering to him, telling him things he didn't want to hear, telling him things that made him do other things, terrible things…

He slid the kitchen instrument into his apron…He mustn't cut himself. That would be bad. Oh, very bad indeed. He couldn't do that yet, no, no. No, not yet. That would come later.

The door opened, and Dora walked in.

There she was, his beautiful golden idol, the one he loved, the one he would always love.

"Are you done yet?" she asked. "My God, you take forever. I've already been across town and back. If it weren't for your laziness, we'd already have the new tiles I need for the bathroom…I can't depend upon you for anything! Margie has a closet full of dresses from Paris, and what do I have?...Rags! Nothing but outdated, out-of-style rags! Oh, my God, you're worthless."

He loved her so much…the bell in her voice, the pouting of her sweet lips…It was all angelic bliss.

He stopped for a moment to gaze upon her heart-stopping beauty.

"What are you grinning at, you ape?" she asked. "Can't you see I'm suffering? My family's coming soon, and all I have is this old green dress. Look at me! This thing is already three months old!"

She was a gem, she was. Such a radiance of intelligence, wisdom, and heart. Boy, what a find!

"I have a surprise for you," he beamed.

Her brow furrowed in that magical way he so loved. Her soul was deep in the throes of love for him, obviously. Her appreciation of his hard work was evident.

"Surprise?" she asked through narrowed eyes. "What surprise?"

"Follow me," he grinned.

The anticipation was killing him. Oh, the joy his surprise would bring!

He motioned her toward the basement door.

"The basement?" she asked. "You've got to be kidding me."

"Please?" he begged. "It will be wonderful. I promise."

"It had better be," she scowled.

She set her shopping bags down on the kitchen floor and pushed past him. She was a take charge kind of woman, she was. She knew when to smack down his foolish ways. Oh, what would he do without her?

She flipped on the basement light and walked into the musty dankness of that underdark. He quickly followed behind, giggling like a schoolgirl with excitement, careful to shut the basement door behind them. Oh, what fun!

In the center of the dark basement was a table they used for various activities. Now it bore his surprise, his wonderful surprise for her, that surprise covered by a wet black bedsheet.

A terrible smell grew overpowering as they approached his work of art.

"What is this?" asked Dora. "What have you got? It smells awful."

"It's a surprise," he explained. "A wonderful surprise. Trust me."

"Is that my silk bedsheet?" she asked, growing anger in her voice. "That *is* my silk bedsheet! You stupid, dumb anim…!"

She touched the edge of the black silk bedsheet, and her voice trailed off in audible surprise. Her face paled, paling to a point where that gorgeous face looked like a mournful maiden's ghost one sees in a painting, haunting but beautiful.

"Th…This is…" she stammered.

She held up her fingers to inspect them, but the red drops on her flawless skin gave her slight pause, a pause that was soon remedied by her own stark fear.

She pulled back from the sheet as if touched by an electric shock. Her fingers were smeared with blood, the crimson liquid smooth in the waxy light of the single basement bulb.

He yanked off the bedsheet as he heard the children singing in the back of his mind:

"Had a wife but couldn't keep her…"

Her face froze in a vision of horror. Her mouth was a round 'O' of a breathless scream…That was how he knew she loved it, loved her surprise.

"Samuel!" she gasped.

Yes, it was Samuel, good old Samuel the fat-cat attorney-at-law, Margie's husband. He was the one you went to if you needed to pull your fat out of the fryer when legal troubles descended upon you, and he was also good for other things…Yes, things like pushing his swollen member in and out of your wife, all the while talking about plans to divorce his own wife and take yours.

It hadn't been too difficult for Margie and Peter to overhear Samuel's plans from inside Samuel's own closet. Peter had stood next to one of the man's tailor-made suits, that suit designed for shattering dreams, that same suit designed to protect Samuel's own interests, all while that same lowlife plowed Peter's wife, a pump, pump, pump, priming the pump for more, always more…Yes, good old Samuel.

Of course, good old Samuel wasn't feeling too well today, no sirree! He was nude, his entrails spilling out, his offensive genitalia removed and set aside, his lifeless eyes staring upwards, his blood everywhere…Yes, he was in a bad way…but, oh, what a surprise he had made!

Of course, Dora didn't exactly see it in the positive light that Peter did…No, she most certainly did not.

She turned to run, but she wasn't going to get far. Oh, no. She wasn't going to make it out of this basement; he would see to that!

Peter pulled out the butcher knife and spun her around.

"Oh, my God, Peter, NO!" she screamed.

And then it was over. The quick slice, the thin line of blood across her pale throat, no way for her to scream anymore…Yes, what a surprise for beautiful Dora. Yes, indeed. She had taste, she did, exquisite taste. Yes, their families would agree on that one soon.

She stumbled backwards as she clutched her slit throat, the blood spraying out in a hot mess all over the basement, a hot mess just like her, a hot mess he was finally cleaning up.

It was time to finish the pies. All he needed to do was prepare the meat, and the baking could begin.

He could hear the singing loud and clear now, much louder, much clearer:

"He put her in a pumpkin shell…"

Yes, he could see it all now. Aunt Grace happily munching on a bit of pie while little Susie skipped rope and sang:

"And there he kept her very well..."

Dora dropped to the basement floor as the last of her life spilled out of her. She choked out a gurgle of blood, and then she was no more.

Peter stared down at her beautiful, still face as comprehension of what he had just done crashed into him. He dropped the knife and heard it clatter across the floor, but his brain did not bother to register this fact; it simply could not.

"Dora?" he choked out.

He knelt down next to his dead wife as his tears spilled from his eyes. Whatever madness had overtaken him, whatever unholy curse had gripped his soul…it was waning now…

But the door to the basement opened.

Peter looked up through blurry eyes to see Margie walking down the basement steps.

She was dressed all in black, a tight and shapely dress to show off her squeezable, yet shapely, form. Her low top exposed the upper mounds of her big beautiful breasts, and the lowcut hem displayed her flawless legs. She was the definition of sex in a bottle.

"There's my big bear," said the woman, a wide and wicked grin upon her beautiful face.

"Dora…I…I…I killed her…" stammered Peter.

"Of course, you did, my dear," smiled Margie. "Why so sad, though? Can't you hear the children, my papa bear?...Can't you hear them singing?"

He could hear them singing, oh, yes, he could:

"Peter, Peter pumpkin eater..."

"No…" breathed out Peter. "No…No, this…You…No, you witch…"

The children grew louder as they sang, the singing louder, pounding into his brain, merciless, unyielding:

"Had another and didn't love her..."

"'Witch' is such a harsh word," said Margie. "I prefer 'Master,' instead."

She stopped in front of him, turned to show him her back, and then lifted her black dress, sliding it seductively up her perfect hips until her bare, heart-shaped bottom was revealed in all its glory.

"Now pledge your affection where it belongs," she commanded.

Peter dropped the bloody knife in his hand and shuffled forward on his knees, his work pants now soaked from his wife's blood, the liquid warmth of that blood a telling trial he struggled across as it soaked through to his knees and legs.

He gripped Margie's beautiful, wide, bare bottom with both hands and kissed the enticing skin of each silky-smooth cheek.

"Samuel had gone on a fishing trip with his wife," said Margie in a sly voice. "They had an accident, and both of them were sliced apart in the propellor. Why, there were whole parts of them that were never found…It's sad, really…Oh, what shall I do without my Samuel?...Oh, yes…I have his money now…But what about Dora's poor husband?...Whatever shall he do? How shall Dora's family take her demise? How shall my Peter explain it to them?...There's nothing to worry about there, my papa bear. I have that all…taken…care of."

Margie let forth a bubbly laugh and then produced a piece of parchment from between her large breasts, a scroll of old and crinkly paper that she unrolled and then placed across her bare butt cheeks.

"Take a look, my papa bear," said Margie. "Look, and you can hear the children singing."

He looked at the scroll laid out across her bare bottom, and he could indeed hear the children singing, that singing loud and clear:

"Peter learned to read and spell…"

He stared at the strange symbols upon the page, but the only thing he recognized was the large pentagram in the center of that page, that page without ink, or rather, that paged inked in blood.

The strange symbols upon the scroll called to him, glowing a sanguine light to match their sanguine composition. He understood now, all of it, and he knew what to do.

"You do know what to do, don't you, my big bear?" asked Margie.

She pulled the scroll away to reveal her bare self once more.

He spread her cheeks and kissed her in her dirtiest place, a pledge of his eternal servitude.

Margie giggled and then shook her head once.

"That never fails to give me a chuckle," she said. "But enough of this groveling. We have to prepare, so hand me the knife, my love."

Peter picked up his dropped butcher knife and passed it to her. She knew what to do with it, oh, yes, she did.

Margie took the blade, sliced open her right index finger, and then pressed her fingerprint into the center of the pentagram upon the blood-inked scroll. She then handed the knife back to Peter and laid the scroll back across her bare bottom.

"Pledge to me in blood, my love," she commanded.

Peter sliced open his own finger and pressed it onto the scroll as well. The scroll lit up in a bright glow of crimson light, and then it was gone, burned away in a flash of spontaneous combustion.

"Yowie!" cried Margie. "I really need to learn to move the contracts away from my bare skin, especially when it's down there."

Peter stared up at her as she turned to stare down at him.

"You're my papa bear forever now," she grinned. "We have work to do, though…That's right…Once your family and once Dora's family eats the pies we make out of our own beloved Dora and Samuel…then I'll take her place, my love. They'll think I'm their Dora, and won't that be grand? I'll have Samuel's money, I'll have my big bear, and I'll have the quiet and loving support of both families…

"I've already had Samuel bequeath all of his money to your former wife. The court will think his money has gone to his 'lover.'…Oh, yes, I'll become Dora, and Dora…will…become…me.

"You see, my love, everyone will think your Dora was Samuel's wife, and we both know his wife was killed in the boating accident right alongside him…Only I will know the truth...It's perfect, isn't it?"

But it wasn't perfect. It wasn't perfect, no…Oh, no, no, no, it wasn't!

Some part of Peter fought against this insanity, this craziness brought down upon him by this witch, this parasite that had wormed her way into his life.

He gripped the butcher knife in his right hand as his facial muscles tensed from the strain of fighting against her. He tried to stand, but willing the action was like trying to swim through mud. He simply could not act against her.

"N…No…" he stammered. "I won't…let you…I…I won't…You can't…do thi—"

"I can do whatever I want, my dear," said Margie with a cold smile. "You see, Samuel served his purpose, and now I've replaced him with you, like I've done with every one of my men for a very, very long time now, ever since the Dark Ages…You belong to me now. Even the children can tell you this one…Can't you hear them singing?...They know the truth, Papa Bear…*I'm* your Dora now."

And he could hear the children singing. He could hear them, but he didn't want to:

"And then he loved her very well."

He understood again, all of it, everything, but this time, he did not fight it. He had been blind before, but now he could see, he could see it all, and in that vision was nothing but his Dora and no one else.

Yes, his Dora was the love of his life. She was so beautiful and smart and kind and wonderful. Her long curly black hair was gorgeous, her dark eyes, mysterious, her hourglass body just an incredible playground of sexual desire.

He kissed her beautiful bare bottom again and gripped her around the legs to nuzzle into her hind end.

"I love you so much, Dora," he grunted out.

"That's my papa bear," smiled his new Dora. "Let's make some pies, shall we?...But first, show me your affection. Kiss me where it counts, Big Bear."

He spread her cheeks and kissed her in her dirtiest place again. Yes, he loved his new Dora very well, very well indeed.

#8…THE LIMINAL

One plus two equals…four? Basic math is just a suggestion, right?

James walked up to the back-alley door and knocked twice. The door was rusted metal with a slat that could open from the other side, something for security, something a guard could look through, but that was because Radditz was paranoid.

He couldn't blame the man. Coco City was a dangerous place, especially down here in the oldest part of the business district. Each city was its own state, and Coco City was no different, though it was better known for thuggery and rogues, but that was fine. James had handled far worse than the human kind of monster.

The slat opened, and a pair of dark eyes gazed upon him.

"State your business," came a rough female voice.

"I need to see Radditz," sighed James. "Just tell him—"

"Oh, it's you!" said the woman behind the door. "Come on in!"

"Wow, that was easy," muttered James.

The door opened after several locks were undone, and James immediately recognized the young black woman guarding the entrance.

"Sofie, right?" he asked.

"Y…Yeah," said the young lady.

James gave her a once-over. It had been a few months since he'd last seen her, but that had been back at Bask.

The young woman was pretty in the face, slender, and had short, pixie-cut, dyed-blonde hair. She was dressed in a utility black jumper with several pockets on the legs, but it was the Ailer 1450 SMG she was strap carrying that held James' attention. The shiny metal fingers of her right hand were tight around the grip of that bullet sprayer.

He walked inside the place, and the young guard shut the door behind him.

"Got your hair cut," he said casually. "I see you got the new arm, too."

"Oh…uhhh…yeah," said Sofie. "Mr. Radditz hooked me up after I got here with Brenda."

"Oh?" asked James. "You're still with Brenda, or did she move on?"

"Oh, no," she replied. "She's still here. She takes care of inventory and reception. She's a bit of a ditz, but—"

"Wait, wait, wait," said James as he shook his head once. "I thought you two were supposed to find work with Isha Corkson. Why are you both working for Radditz?"

"Mr. Radditz took us in," shrugged Sofie. "I wasn't going to turn him down. I don't shoot a gift bird in flight."

"Gift bird…" said James as he rolled his eyes. "It should be gift horse…You know what? Doesn't matter…Where is the old lech?"

"Mr. Radditz?" asked Sofie. "He's in back…Is there something wrong? Do you have artifacts you want to move or something you want repaired?"

"Not at all," sighed James. "I was just stopping by. I actually stopped by to see where the old dog had sent you two, or if you two had even made it here."

"Really?" smiled Sofie.

"Yeah," said James. "How are you holding up? How's that arm working out for you?"

She frowned as she lowered her gaze to look at the new cyber-rune arm that had replaced her real one. James could see the haunted look in her dark eyes, not surprising considering what she had already been through.

"The arm is fine," said Sofie in a quiet voice. "I…still have trouble sleeping at night, though. That thing that killed all my friends…"

"Yeah," grunted James.

She turned her gaze back upon James and frowned again.

"The Death Fairies were the first group of people that made me feel like I belonged," she said unhappily. "We thought we were unstoppable…They were my friends…and then some giant wolf killed them all."

"You can't dwell on it," said James. "You shouldn't forget them—never do that—but at some point you have to continue living your life."

"I know…" sighed Sofie. "Working here has helped me with that, and Brenda, ditz that she is, has helped me with that, too…She has a fear of cultists now, though."

"Yeah," snorted James. "That's a good thing. She'll live longer."

"Yeah," smiled Sofie. "We're definitely better off here."

"Well…" shrugged James. "I had to check to make sure you two were okay. I should still see Radditz, though. He needs to know I'm in town."

She gave him a mild punch on the arm with her left hand.

"Awww…You old softie," she chuckled. "Head on back, old timer. I have to stay up front until I'm off duty, but I'm glad you stopped by. You did save my life, after all."

"Thanks," grunted James.

He headed down a narrow hallway that had two doors along the west side to his right and a door at the south end, all three doors simple brown wood with frosted glass windows set within them.

"And I'm not that old!" called back James.

He heard the young woman chuckle as he stepped up to the south door. He opened the south door and walked into a small receptionist's office.

"This is new," he said in strange interest.

The small room had freshly-painted white walls with a small wooden desk at the back end of it, two wooden doors behind that desk, one on each side of it. Upon that desk was a brand-new rune-tech computer, and behind that computer, sitting in a grey swivel chair, was Brenda.

Unlike Sofie, the young woman did not look that much different from the first time James had seen her. The young white woman possessed a cute round face with a button nose and dark eyes. She had her short black hair in a bowl cut, and she wore the same kind of utility black jumper that Sofie sported, so at least Radditz was consistent in attempting to hide his lechery.

The young lady looked up at James, but her dark eyes widened as she recognized him.

"Oh, it's you!" she said with a wide smile.

"Yep," smirked James. "I already got that reaction from Sofie."

"I'm so glad you're back!" replied Brenda. "I didn't think I'd see you again!"

"Oh, the old man is my buyer," snorted James. "I have to come here to sell. Not to mention that he's the best damned rune-technician and mechanic around."

"Oh, I know that," nodded Brenda. "Mr. Radditz has been teaching me some of the trade. I've been learning rune wiring. He's been really kind to us."

James could envision Brenda bent over a piece of rune-tech, her big heart-shaped bottom in the air, the old man staring right down at that butt from behind her.

"I'll bet he has," snorted James as he shook his head. "I stopped by to check on you and Sofie, but I can see you're doing fine. However, I should let Radditz know I'm in town. Sofie said he's in back, but...he must have remodeled the place."

"Oh, yeah," nodded Brenda. "He put in this office after he took us in. He redid the guard's office, too."

"Uh, huh," said James. "Well...I'll just head on back then. I already know my way around."

"Are you going to be in town for long?" asked Brenda.

"Probably not," sighed James. "We'll see."

"Oh..." said Brenda, but she sounded disappointed.

"Tell you what..." said James. "We'll all go out to dinner later, okay? I think the old man will agree to that."

"That would be great!" smiled Brenda. "I'll tell Sofie."

"Yeah," replied James. "She'll be happy to hear that, I think. Anyway, I'm gonna go see Radditz for a bit."

"Okay, Mr. James," grinned Brenda. "Just head through the left door behind me...Uhhh...Your left, not mine."

"Got it," nodded James.

He walked through the left door and into Radditz's shop.

Back in his younger days, he'd have gone after either one of those girls, probably both at the same time, but he was pushing fifty now, and those young ladies were half his age. His dark skin was weathered, his short curly black hair had flecks of grey in it, and of course, he had that scar running from right underneath his left eye all the way down to the bottom of his chin...Nah...He wasn't chasing tail anymore. He was out of that game.

No, he had everything he needed already on him. He kept his clothing simple in look and style: a black-T, brown work pants with pockets, his brown leather jacket, his black bullet-proof vest, his enchanted steel neck collar that contained his helmet, and his good brown leather hiking boots...That clothing was his home.

His clothes were enchanted to Hell and back, imbued with mage armor, self-repair, self-cleaning, and pockets with the Deep enchantment, so everything he needed was already on him...not to mention his Rune Maker and his cavalry saber. Those were his protection, and you could never have enough protection in this crazy world of magic and monsters.

He shook his head free of those thoughts as he walked across the large garage and up to the inventory desk where Radditz was currently sorting through acquired artifacts the old man was going to move on the black market.

Lazarus Radditz was a big white man, six-foot-four, with broad shoulders and more muscle than a sixty-two-year-old had a right to have. The right side of his bald head was limned with sweat, while the left above his lips was all rune-tech steel, a big ruby goggle where his left eye should have been. He was dressed in a grease-stained white tank top, and he looked up and grinned at James through a bushy grey beard.

"James, you lazy piece of—" he began.

"Stow it," snorted James. "I'm not taking guff from a man with the same last name as a minor *Dragon Ball* villain."

"Sorry," shrugged Radditz. "Don't get the reference. If you're going to insult someone, it's at least got to be understandable. I guess things were way different in that universe you came from, huh?"

James rolled his eyes. Radditz was one of the few people that knew James was a Rift Walker, that James had wandered through a rift and had ended up in this universe, but that was because the old man could detect different rift signatures with that ruby eye of his.

"Yeah, yeah," replied James. "Look, I just stopped by to inquire about the two young women I sent your way. I wanted to make sure they were all right, and I thought you would have sent them Isha's way by now, but it looks like you got greedy, didn't you, you old lech? They're less than half your age, you know."

"Hey, if there's grass on the field, play ball," shrugged Radditz. "I think you told me that once."

"Out of all the things I've said, *that's* what you remember?" asked James as he shook his head.

"Eh," shrugged the older man. "Doesn't matter…You in town for a while?"

"Yeah," said James. "I told the girls we could all go out to eat together before I leave."

"Who's paying?" asked Radditz.

"I'll pay for them," frowned James. "You can pay for yourself."

"Yeah, yeah," grunted the older man. "Look, I'll tell you what. If you do a little job for me, you can make a little money, *and* I'll pay for dinner. How's that sound?"

"That depends," snorted James. "What's the job?"

He knew better than to just accept a job with no questions asked. Life was way too dangerous in this world to do that.

"I got a couple of freelancers that were hired by Isha to check out a building here in Coco," said Radditz.

"When you say freelancers, you're not talking about the girls, are you?" asked James through narrowed eyes.

He wasn't their father, but he also didn't want them doing that kind of work. Mercenary work had a short life-expectancy.

"Nah, nah," said the older man as he waved off James. "My sister's kid and his friend want to dip into your line of work."

"And you didn't warn them off?" asked James. "Ain't he family, man? That's your nephew…What the hell?"

"That's where you come in," grunted Radditz. "This job Isha's got set up should be a breeze for you. It's an abandoned building right here in the B.D. There's a rumor going around that some junkies disappeared in it. Coco State of Affairs is paying a little for someone to go check it out, so just go check it out, watch their backs, and wave 'em off this life…

"Show 'em your ugly face and that scar of yours. Tell 'em that Widow story and about some of the other things you've come across. Tell 'em about the Minotaur of Park Ridge."

"Yeah, I see what you want," grunted James. "Okay, I guess I can swing that. Where is this place I'm supposed to go?"

"It's over at Garden Gable," said Radditz. "Junkie Town. It's not technically in the business district, but it's close enough. You know where that is?"

"Yeah," said James. "I know it…Where are these kids of yours anyway?"

"I'll get ahold of 'em," grunted Radditz. "Head over to my sister's, pick 'em up, get this done, and then we'll all go out to eat."

"Yeah, all right," said James. "Works for me."

"Yeah, get it done, and do it right this time, you lazy son of a—" started the older man.

"Don't go there," snorted James. "I'm not taking heat from a *Cowboy Bebop* wannabe."

"Still don't get the reference, man," grinned Radditz.

*****

James and his two new companions headed down the short flight of wide, cracked, concrete steps that led to a rusty, grey, metal door. The stairs were in-between two dank rain-stained walls of cracked concrete, and the door in question had the words "ONLY THE DEAD WALK HERE" spraypainted across it in big red letters.

"Now you two follow my lead," said James. "If anything goes down, find cover *first*. Don't stand around like idiots waiting to get shot or jumped. If there is no cover, unload a clip in it...Seriously. Point is, don't get killed on my watch."

He took a brief moment to study the two young men.

Both were in their early twenties, both skinny dorks with two braincells between them, but they were family as far as James was concerned, because any family of Radditz's was also the closest thing James had to family anymore. His own family was long dead...something he did not wish to dwell on any longer than he had to.

Morgan was the bolder of the two, a slender young man with mid-length, greasy, black hair and a big, awkward-looking, hawk nose to match his dark-brown eyes. He had on a generic black leather jacket with punk studs on the shoulders, a black Tee, black denim jeans, and black work boots. He looked like a kid who was trying too hard to be cool. All he needed were the slimline shades and the black duster to look like a Neo-from-*The-Matrix* wannabe.

Ethan, on the other hand, was a tall skinny kid with regular glasses on his pointed nose. This kid had on a plain, unadorned, brown bomber jacket, a blue Tee, tan slacks, and brown hiking boots. He looked like a college nerd that had joined an extracurricular activity way outside of his competency.

James took a look at their gear. Both were packing Jacobs-Brill light SMGs, model 745s. They both had ammo belts with color-coded pockets, so at least they had that much in common sense.

"Do either one of you have any shooting experience?" asked James.

"We hit the range every week," nodded Morgan. "We've got plenty of experience in small arms."

"Oh, yeah?" asked James. "What ammo have you got?"

"Ifrit, Ymir, and Raijin rounds," said Ethan. "I figured that would cover the basics. It's tougher to get ahold of the more expensive types without getting a state license…What kind are you carrying?"

"Normal bullets," said James.

"What!" snorted Morgan. "I thought you were some kind of badass. That's what Uncle Laz told us anyway."

"I don't need anything but normal bullets," grimaced James. "It's because I have this, kid."

James drew his six-shooter and held it up so that both of them could see it, specifically the runes etched along the barrel.

"That's a Rune Maker!" breathed Ethan in obvious recognition. "I didn't think any of those were still around!"

"A Rune Maker?" asked Morgan.

"It enchants bullets when they're fired," said Ethan. "It's a revolver, and it only holds six rounds at a time, but Mr. James doesn't need anything but normal bullets for it. Each sigil on a Rune Maker stamps the runes onto the bullets when they exit the chamber."

"That sounds handy," said Morgan. "Why don't they make more of these? They should do that with submachine guns and assault rifles."

"It's too expensive and too dangerous," said Ethan as he shook his head. "Only a few Rune Makers were ever made. It takes a pact with a demon to make one."

"No kidding?" asked James.

That he had not known about his museum piece.

"Well, what do you know," said James as he scrunched up his lips. "You learn something new every day…Look, you two, I may not know everything, but I do know my business, so I suggest you two follow my lead and learn some things, okay?"

The two young men stared at each other for a brief second and then turned their attention back upon James as James holstered his weapon.

James had on his brown leather driving gloves, and he pointed his gloved right index finger at Morgan's face.

"And I am a badass," frowned James. "There's a reason I'm in charge right now. It's because 'Uncle Laz' doesn't want to see either one of you with your brains blown out all over the walk."

"We don't need a babysitter," frowned Morgan.

"No, you need a drill sergeant," continued James, "but since we don't have one, you'll have to settle for me. You follow my lead, listen to what I say, and hopefully, things will go smoothly."

"Hopefully?" asked Ethan. "I thought this was just a training job."

"It is," nodded James. "This is a green-letter pick from Isha, and that means almost anyone can do it, but you know what I've learned from doing Isha's jobs? Hell, you know what I've learned from doing any job in this godforsaken world?"

"What?" asked Morgan in a cautious tone.

"Always expect the worst," frowned James. "That advice will keep you alive longer than anything else."

"That's kind of cynical," said Ethan.

"Did you read the warning on the door?" said James. "I've seen people melted into puddles of goo by things that are all eyes, tentacles, and teeth. I wouldn't say I'm cynical; I'd say I'm realistic."

"Uh, huh," said Morgan. "It's an abandoned building in Junkie Town. I stepped over a wino passed out in his own vomit on the way here."

"Yeah," grunted James. "Hopefully, you'll step back over him on the way back."

"Whatever," frowned Morgan.

"Look," said James firmly. "You just follow my lead. I know rules to this crap that you haven't learned yet…For one thing, it's a good thing we're going in with three people and not four."

"Huh?" asked Ethan. "Why's that?"

"The number four is bad luck in this business," said James. "Remember that…Anyway, let's just get this done. All we have to do is sweep the building and look for evidence about what happened to these missing homeless people. I'll teach you some tricks of the trade along the way. You'll live longer."

Morgan frowned at him, but Ethan simply nodded his head in compliance.

"Okay," said Ethan.

"Good," said James. "Guns ready."

He reached up and pressed a button on his steel neck collar, and his Hermes-Alliette retractable helm raised up to completely cover his head and face. The banded helm came with a corrugated breathing mask, a pair of amber visors for enhanced vision, and its own combat virtual intelligence…He had relied on it many times in the past. Besides, he wanted to impress these two newbs, even though that was kind of juvenile, but these pretentious little dinks needed to learn which one of the three of them had actually been around the block…Spoilers: it wasn't them.

James drew his Rune Maker and held the barrel upright as he reached for the handle of the rusty grey door before them. His piece was loaded, he had his saber sheathed on his left hip, and as green as the two young men behind him were, they were still his backup, so he was ready to go in.

He turned the old metal knob, opened the door, and stepped into the building, his two new "pupils" right behind him.

The door shut behind them, but James was too busy studying his surroundings to be concerned with that.

"What the…?" he breathed out.

They were in a parking garage, a big one, one so large he couldn't see the actual end of it. It just kind of traveled off into a horizon of darkness, long, flickering, fluorescent lamps lighting the way in a line overhead.

"This is inside an abandoned building?" asked Sofie.

James ignored her.

He swiveled to look behind himself, peering past all three of his companions, but there was no door anymore. The rusty, grey, metal door was gone, replaced by a horizon of darkness lit by long, flickering, fluorescent lamps, an endless parking garage. It was as if they had walked through a rift portal, but his helmet VI hadn't informed him of such, so that couldn't be it. He had no idea where they were.

"This is…problematic," muttered James.

A quick inspection revealed cars along each side of the lane they were in, cars from *his* world, James' world, not this one. There were Fords, Chevys, GMs, Toyotas, and even a light-blue Mustang, but this only heightened his anxiety over the matter. They couldn't be in his original world…That place was long gone, rubble and ash.

"This is definitely not right," said James in a low voice.

"Where is this?" asked Ethan.

"What are these weird cars?" asked Morgan. "They have wheels."

"They don't run on magic," replied James. "They run on a fossil fuel, gasoline. They don't hover like the cars you're used to."

"Gasoline?" asked Ethan. "What's that?"

"It's made from crude oil," said James. "It burns in the…You know what? Not important. Point is, we're not where we're supposed to be."

"Where are we, then?" asked Sofie.

"No idea," frowned James, though they couldn't see his expressions behind his helmet. "Just keep on alert. Something's definitely not right. We need to get out of here."

"How do we do that?" asked Ethan. "The door's gone."

"Yep," grunted James. "Guess we'll start walking…There's got to be some clue as to what is going—"

But he was cut short by a loud screech that echoed across the vast garage.

"Something's in here with us," said Sofie.

The young woman held up her Ailer SMG as she spun in place to locate the source of the sudden noise. Her dark eyes were wide, and James could visibly see the slight panic pulsing through her.

"Three rules, kids," he said unhappily. "Rule Number One: There's always something in one of these places, and it's always in here with you…Rule Number Two: It will find you."

Another loud shriek echoed across the garage, but it was louder this time, closer.

"W…What's Rule Number Three?" asked Morgan in a tremulous voice.

"When it finds you…kill it," said James.

He pulled back the hammer on his Rune Maker. The loud click made by the enchanted pistol was deafening in the sudden silence as everyone held their breath. That silence was broken by Ethan's nervous voice, a hushed whisper that still sounded incredibly loud in their quiet surroundings.

"There's someone there…" said the young man.

James swiveled and did a quick study of the person in the distance. He could see the individual in his HUD, but this person did not register any warning or radiant aura from his VI.

The individual in the distance looked like a man in a brown trench coat, a brown fedora on his head, his head lowered to where only the top of his hat could be seen.

"Hey!" yelled James. "State your business!"

This person gradually raised his head to reveal his face, and…

The face beneath the hat was a grinning skull, but it was more than that, for this skull had two pristine eyes in the orbital sockets, though what color those eyes were, James could not tell from this distance.

The skull-man opened its creaking jaws and let forth another high-pitched shriek, and the sound of it was a booming echo around the dark parking garage. James' young crew immediately covered their ears, but James' helmet initiated automatic sonic protection for his own ears, so he didn't have to worry about that.

"It…It can't be!" stammered Morgan. "It's the Shrieker!"

"Waste it!" yelled James. "Ifrit's Rage!"

His command lit up the flame sigil upon his pistol. He leveled his Rune Maker, pulled the trigger, and the sound of the "BANG!" echoed around the garage.

This creature, this "Shrieker," disappeared from sight, only to reappear right in front of him.

"Oh, shi—" began James, but a punch to the chest by a skeletal fist cut short that expletive.

He went flying backwards to skid on his back across the garage pavement, his gun slipping from his grasp to slide across pavement as well. The impact temporarily took his breath, but even as old as he was, he was used to being knocked around, so this only stopped him for a few brief seconds.

He struggled to stand as he watched his companions scatter, and his breath came back to him as he barked out a quick warning the moment it did.

"It's got super speed!" he yelled. "Watch your aim! Don't shoot each other in the crossfire!"

A thick black leather boot kicked him in the right side of his helmet, and his HUD temporarily went crazy. Skeletal fingers clutched him around the throat as he was picked up from the garage floor, picked up like a child's toy to dangle in this thing's powerful, icy grip.

James could see the creature's bright blue eyes now, ocean-blue eyes set within the orbital sockets of the skull, and that skull was not a mask; of that, he was certain.

It shrieked in his face, its jaws creaking wide open, and he could see a long and pointed tongue in its mouth, but unlike his young and green companions, this did not shake him. He'd seen far worse.

He reached down and tapped the flame rune on his bulletproof vest with his left gloved hand. The rune glowed a bright red as the protective flame barrier it evoked began to build in its familiar orange, egg-shaped, hexagonal pattern, but that pattern was interrupted as the creature chucked James like a horseshoe away from itself.

James rolled across the parking-garage floor yet again, but this time his barrier shorted out before it could fully build. It flickered into existence for a brief second, and then it was gone, a safety feature built into the enchantment to keep James from being fried by his own barrier.

"Somebody, shoot it!" he croaked out.

Gunshots rang out as orange-glowing bullets whizzed by him overhead.

The creature took off at such speed that it vanished from James' vision, only to reappear in front of Ethan. It gripped Ethan's right wrist to where the boy could not fire, and the young man cried out in pain as the bones in his wrist began to feel the pressure of breaking.

This thing withdrew a small black bar from its trench coat, and a "SHING!" sound rang out as it flicked forth a small but deadly switchblade. It brought the blade up to Ethan's terrified face, right next to the young man's neck, ready to plunge the small shaft of steel into the boy's left carotid.

"Let him go!" yelled Morgan.

James had not expected such a protest to work, but the creature tossed Ethan aside like so much garbage, and the young man with glasses bounced off of the nearest car to roll across garage-floor pavement.

The creature turned its attention upon Morgan.

The boy was sitting on his rump as if he had fallen over, but he had his SMG in the air, pointed directly at this "Shrieker," though both of his hands were shaking.

James staggered to his feet, but he was still a little out of it, so he stumbled and fell to his knees…What he really needed to do was get to his gun before that thing killed one of the people he was in charge of protecting…He didn't want to lose a single one of them. There was a reason he usually didn't work with others.

He needed to do something, so he did the only thing he could at the moment.

"Shoot it, Morgan!" he yelled.

The creature slowly walked forward toward Morgan, stared down at him with those weird blue eyes, and then let forth another menacing shriek.

Perhaps it was the shriek that startled the young man into action, or perhaps it was James' command, but Morgan cried out once and then pulled the trigger of his Jacobs-Brill 745. The light SMG rattled off a burst of enchanted bullets, and those bullets proceeded to riddle the trench coat and chest area of this skeletal thing.

The creature jerked backwards as it was struck multiple times, and then its body lit up in a wreath of flame, set aflame by Morgan's loaded Ifrit rounds, its form a pyre of burning bones and cloth as it fell to the pavement a second later.

James was finally able to get to his feet. He stood, walked over to his Rune Maker, picked it up, and took in a couple of deep breaths through his helm's filter.

He turned to look at the pile of ash that Morgan's "Shrieker" had left behind.

"What was that thing?" asked Sofie as she helped Ethan get to his feet.

"No idea," muttered James. "Morgan seemed to know, though…What was that thing, Morgan?"

The young man slowly stood, turned, and immediately threw up…Well, that was actually a good sign. Maybe this life wasn't for him after all.

James waited for the young man to finish.

Morgan wiped his lips clean on the sleeve of his black leather jacket, turned, and shook his head once.

"That was the Shrieker," he said in a shaky voice. "Harriet Elloss told me the story about that thing when I was a kid to scare me…That story gave me nightmares…but…but she made it up. I know she did…It's not real."

"Well…clearly it was," grunted James.

"Harriet Elloss?" asked Ethan. "Wasn't she that girl that used to live next to you?"

"Yeah," nodded Morgan. "Her family moved away to Hollowstone when we were kids."

"That's not important," said James unhappily. "Look, you can all reminisce later. What I want to know right now is why no one took a shot. You don't take a shot when you have it, you won't get another chance to…You'll be dead…And that goes double for you, Sofie. You've got more experience than these two combined. Why didn't you shoot?"

"Yeah," asked Ethan. "What were you doing?"

"I couldn't get a shot lined up," frowned Sofie. "I would have hit one of you two."

"All right, all right," grunted James. "Let's not split hairs. We need to find our way out of here and report back to Isha. I still don't know where we are, and considering most pocket universes collapse after their master is destroyed, that thing, that Shrieker, wasn't the boss of this place."

"Pocket universe?" asked Ethan.

"Yeah," said James. "We must have crossed into one. They're typically traps, like when a fly gets caught in a spider's web. We have to find the mastermind behind it, or we'll be stuck here until we do…Green-letter job, my a—"

"Let's just keep moving," said Sofie. "We need to find an exit, just like Mr. James said…Hmm…Maybe one of these cars works. We could always—"

"Doubtful," said James. "Highly doubtful they function at all. We can try one of them, but I think it would be a waste of time."

"I don't know," frowned Sofie. "I kind of like that Mustang over there..."

"A light-blue Mustang is an atrocity," chuckled James. "I don't think so. Even so, unless you know how to hotwire a car from another universe, none of these vehicles will do us much good."

"Yeah, but—" started Sofie, but she didn't get to finish her sentence.

"Quiet!" hissed Ethan. "Do you hear that?"

James listened for a second, and his helmet's audio picked up a clicking sound, like high heels on pavement, and then it grew louder as multiple clicking noises erupted from the direction of the light-blue Mustang.

"Everybody, ready," said James. "Back away toward me…"

A huge scarlet-coated beetle the size of a small dog appeared upon the roof of the Mustang, then another on the hood, then another on the roof, and then the windows of the vehicle shattered as a swarm of these overgrown insects burst out from the interior of the car.

The first of the beetles crawled off the car to the garage pavement and spit a line of liquid that immediately set aflame as that line traversed the distance between James' little group and the beetle itself.

They all backed up to keep from being struck by the flaming spit, and the parking-garage floor lit up as a pool of the burning liquid congealed right in front of them.

"F…Fire beetles!" yelled Ethan, but the boy sounded panicked, not altogether there.

"Ymir's Breath!" cried James.

His Rune Maker's frost sigil lit up with a cold blue light.

"Everybody, switch to Ymir rounds!" he yelled.

He fired off two shots in succession, both at two different beetles, and the giant red scarabs ceased moving as they coated over with frost at the same time.

The rest of his group opened fire as multiple lines of flaming spit came sailing toward them all.

A swarm of these things came over the Mustang as James fired off three more rounds and then quick-loaded his pistol.

He looked over toward Sofie, but she simply stood there trying to get her clip out of her Ailer SMG.

"Gun's jammed!" she yelled.

"Give me that!" snapped James.

James holstered his Rune Maker as Sofie undid the shoulder strap of her weapon. She flipped her gun to him, he slammed the butt end of the long clip at the bottom of the SMG onto his right leg, the type-indicator-light for the rounds lit up in glorious blue, and then James opened fire.

A spray of deadly frost rounds annihilated another row of beetles.

"Keep firing!" commanded James.

The two young men off to his right obeyed this time, and they unloaded their clips into the deadly swarm until not one of the overgrown insects remained alive.

James flipped the spent SMG back to Sofie and shook his head once.

"You didn't make sure the clip was all the way in," he frowned. "You can't eject it once it's past the locking bar, and the gun won't fire until the first bullet is in the chamber. It has to read the bullet type in order for the indicator light to activate, and if the indicator light doesn't activate, you can't take the clip out…One more reason I don't like the Ailer brand."

If it wasn't one thing, it was another, but this was getting out of hand. It was clear he couldn't protect them as well as he'd first thought he could…It had never been his intention to take them into an actual combat zone. They needed to get out of here, and quickly.

But Ethan completely ignored James' little chewing-out of Sofie. The young man swallowed hard and shook his head a couple of times instead.

"Those were fire beetles," said Ethan in a shaky voice. "They're only supposed to live in volcanoes. My grandpa told me about them…They'll burn you to death and then eat your charred flesh. My grandpa saw it happen. When I was five, he told me all about this guy who died right in front of him, about the beetles swarming all over the guy while he was still on fire…That story…That story terrified me."

Something clicked in James' brain at that moment. It was an epiphany of sorts, though he didn't yet have it all figured out.

"Wait, what did you say?" he asked. "Did you say you were scared of them?"

"Y…Yeah," stammered Ethan. "I never thought I'd actually see one, though…"

"And normally you wouldn't," said James. "I think I know what's going on here…but if that's the case…then the next thing up will be a giant…"

The flickering lights above their heads suddenly dimmed, though they continued to flicker. The shadows around them grew thicker as a sibilant whispering picked up from all around them.

James saw the dark figure rise from out of a pool of shadows, a slender and dark form that rose to a full height of over six-and-a-half-feet.

The man that stepped forward was dressed in banded black soldier armor, a black duster, and thick black boots. On his face was a combat infantry mask with a black visor and a corrugated breather, and around that mask was long black hair that flowed and moved as if by its own volition, like tendrils of living shadow.

"I was wrong!" barked James. "Run!"

But his companions never got the chance to.

The man in black raised his hand, that hand covered by thick black soldier's armor, a metal gauntlet with serrated ridges, and Morgan was suddenly knocked off his feet to slide on his back across the garage floor.

Ethan raised his own SMG to fire, but a black tentacle of inky darkness sprouted from a nearby shadow to whip across his right wrist. The young man cried out as his bones actually broke this time, his right arm bending at an odd angle from the force of the blow.

Sofie backed away until she was behind James, but James did not move. There was nowhere to go in here anyway, and he knew that now.

"Don't do this, Jack!" yelled James.

The tall and slender man in black reached up with his left hand toward his mask, and James knew exactly what he was going to do, something James simply could not allow.

"Sorry, Jack," frowned James. "Ymir's Breath."

The ice sigil on his Rune Maker glowed a bright blue as he drew the pistol at blinding speed. He had already reloaded the weapon, so he had all six shots.

He fired off three rounds squarely into the armored chest plate of the tall dark man before him. The rounds impacted upon their target, and then the man in black coated over with a fine sheet of white hoarfrost, covered from head to toe in the blinding white of magic cold.

"Banshee's Wail," said James.

A sigil on his pistol lit up in neon purple, and James fired a single round at his currently frozen opponent. The bullet lodged in the ice, there was a high-pitched whine as the round activated, and then a sonic sphere of destruction emanated outwards, shattering the figure into so many dark, frozen shards.

James cursed under his breath and shook his head in anger. Yeah, he definitely knew what was going on now, and it was not what he had first thought it had been. No, what was actually going on had just pushed all of his buttons at once.

Ethan cried out in pain as he clutched his right arm and held the broken limb close to himself.

"What was that?" asked Morgan. "What is going on here! Where are these things coming from! How do we get out of here!"

"Calm down," said James firmly. "I know where we are now."

Sofie walked past him and gave him an odd look.

"Oh?" she asked. "You do?"

"Yeah," replied James. "We're not in a pocket universe."

"Where are we, then?" asked Sofie. "Do you even know where we are?"

"Yeah," grunted James. "We're in the Liminal."

"What?" winced Ethan. "Are you serious?"

"Yeah," said James.

"The Liminal?" asked Morgan. "What's the Liminal? Is it a pocket universe?"

"It's not a pocket universe," said James unhappily. "A pocket universe wouldn't have our worst nightmares in it…No, the Liminal is an entirely different plane of existence."

"I didn't…didn't think it was real," said Ethan as he gritted his teeth in pain.

"Oh, it's real, and we're in it," said James.

"That still doesn't explain what it is," said Morgan.

"It's a realm that borders the Umbra," said James. "The Umbra is the Shadow World, Death's realm. The Liminal is on the edge of it. The Liminal brings your greatest fears to life and pits them against you. That's what's been going on…We're actually being attacked by our own fears, and those fears don't have to exist in the real world to be real in here."

"I knew it…" breathed Morgan. "I knew the Shrieker wasn't real."

"How do we get out?" asked Ethan. "You said these pocket universes have a master, but if this isn't a pocket universe…"

"Oh, the Liminal has a master," frowned James. "It has a master, and I know who it is."

"Really?" asked Sofie. "Who is it?"

"You see, Jack is *my* fear," explained James. "There's no way in Hell I'd be able to kill Jack the way I did, because aside from being damn-near unkillable, Jack isn't real. He's the culmination of a little girl's fears—a powerful little girl, true—but he's not real.

"He's a mix of the Boogeyman, Spring-Heeled Jack, and Slenderman, none of which are real. I know I've said 'everything's real' in the past, but not everything is. Jack is something Maria brought to life in order to protect herself, and Maria's not here, so…"

"So he can't be here, either," winced Ethan. "I understand...Who's Maria?"

"Doesn't matter," said James unhappily. "You see, Jack has the powers of all three creatures I mentioned, which is why he tore into us so quickly. He can breathe fire, walk through shadows, control darkness, and move stuff with his mind through telekinesis. If he takes off his mask and you see his face...you die of fright...but like I said, Jack isn't real. Yeah, yeah, I know he's got that Darth Vader look going for him, especially when he uses his telekinesis. Am I right, Sofie?"

"So he fell to the Dark Side?" asked the young woman.

"Jack is the Dark Side," said James, "but that's not my point."

"None of what you said makes any sense," said Morgan. "I don't understand what you're talking about."

"Exactly," grunted James. "And to be fair, you shouldn't. You see, four is a bad luck number because it's Death's number. I've thought about it a lot, and I would have never come into this 'building' with three other people. There's no way I'd do that, because I'm not stupid. The one thing I've learned in this business is that four people in a party is as bad of luck as you get."

"What does that mean?" asked Sofie.

"It means one of us is a liar," explained James. "One of us...isn't real."

"What?" asked Ethan. "But that's not possible...is it?"

"It is if we're in the Liminal," said James. "This place is built on lies. It's meant to raise your hackles and bring out your deepest fears so that it can consume you, suck you away into the Umbra. I'm pretty sure now that the master of this place is here with us."

"Here with us?" asked Morgan.

"Yeah," said James. "One of us isn't real...because one of us is Death himself."

The two young men looked each other over, carefully studying every detail about the other.

"You see, all of us faced our fears," continued James, "only one of us didn't...No, one of us got skipped...Isn't that right, Sofie?"

James turned to look upon the young woman, but she shook her head in denial.

"If what you said about this place is true," she replied, "then my fear hasn't shown up yet."

"And it won't," said James. "It won't, because you don't know what it is."

"I…I do too," stammered Sofie.

"I know what she's afraid of," replied James, "but you don't because she's not here, and you're not her. So tell me, 'Sofie,' what are you afraid of?"

"I…I don't want to talk about it," said Sofie.

"Whoa…" said Morgan nervously. "Are you sure about this, Mr. James? I mean, I think we're all real…We have to be…If she doesn't want to talk about her greatest fear…"

He stopped talking as James shook his head no.

"No, there's no way you could know what the Dark Side of the Force is, Sofie," he said firmly. "The real Sofie has never even heard of *Star Wars*…She's also never seen any cars like this before, so there's no way she could know what a Mustang is, either."

"What are you talking about?" asked Ethan. "I don't understand…"

"Exactly," said James. "You wouldn't, and you shouldn't. That was my point…So, what are you afraid of Sofie? What can we expect to hit us in here?"

"Yeah," winced Ethan. "Tell us so we can be ready."

"Just tell him, Sofie," said Morgan. "He'll leave you alone if you tell him."

"Yeah, why don't you tell me, 'Sofie,'" grimaced James. "Or should I say, 'Death'?...This was a trap you set up just for me, isn't it? You couldn't kill me back in the old world, so you decided to get me here…but all of this is some B.S., isn't it? You don't have permission to take me, do you?...It's not my time, and you know it. You have to do it on the sly, which is why you set up this little trap.

"It's because I traveled with Jack, and you just can't let that go, can you? I know, because the phone I have let me see what happened to them after I was gone, and you were always there, always chasing them. That's why you brought up that cheap imitation of Jack, but that was your mistake, because that reminded me of Maria, and I'll never get to see her again, so all you've done is piss me off…No, you're not getting any fear from me, so all you're doing is shooting blanks…Now stop screwing with us and let us go."

The young black woman looked at Ethan, then at Morgan, and then back at James. She looked thoughtful for a moment, smiled, and then shook her head no.

"I guess it's not your time after all, is it, James?" she said as her voice deepened to that of a man's.

The lights dimmed as she grew in form and size, growing and darkening as the parking-garage lights receded at the same time.

The two young men under James' protection paled in complexion as the figure before them took shape.

James turned his gaze aside so that he could only see out of his peripheral.

"Don't look at him!" warned James. "Don't look directly at him!"

The figure before him radiated a terrifying aura of both fear and death. James fixed his gaze on the otherworldy creature's skeletal left hand, and that hand pointed one bony finger behind them.

"Both of you turn around," ordered James. "Turn around, and don't look back. Don't look at him. Just follow me."

He turned and made sure his two charges did as well. He guided the both of them toward the glowing red exit sign in the distance, a neon sign hanging from the ceiling that had simply manifested while they had not been looking, that sign guiding them both toward the rusty, grey, metal door they had originally come in through.

"Keep walking," commanded James. "Just keep walking and don't look back. Don't fall for any of that Orpheus crap. Don't say anything, don't look back, and just keep walking. He's letting us leave."

He holstered his Rune Maker and put both of his gloved hands on the back of his charges' heads. He did not want them turning around. He did not want them to so much as turn their empty heads.

"Just keep moving," he ordered.

They made it to the door beneath the lit exit sign, Morgan turned the rusty doorknob upon that door with one trembling hand, and all three of them exited without further delay.

The door shut behind them as they stepped back onto the cracked concrete steps they had originally walked down to get to this cursed building.

"Wh…What just happened?" asked Morgan.

"You met Death, boys," snorted James. "That's the kind of crap you have to put up with in this line of work."

"Oh…" said Morgan in a quiet voice.

"Now, come on," said James. "We have to get Ethan, here, to a hospital, and then I have a dinner to attend."

"Oh…" said Morgan again.

James could tell the young man was in slight shock.

"Hey, on the bright side, you completed the job," said James. "Look…"

He opened the grey door again, and both boys flinched as they stared into the darkness of an empty, abandoned building.

"Death will set up shop somewhere else," said James. "You probably won't be seeing him again for…hopefully…a very long time. He wasn't after you anyway…Now…I think I speak for all of us when I say, 'let's get the hell out of here.'"

He let the door swing shut, and both young men said nothing as they trudged up the concrete steps and back into the proper of Garden Gable.

Yeah, James wasn't worried about these two anymore. The fight was definitely out of them, and they wouldn't be taking up the mercenary life any time soon.

Radditz would be pleased, of course, but James was none too happy about the experience. He did not like to be reminded of his former life, though he dwelled on it often, but that was something he dealt with one day at a time.

No, he had a new life to lead anyway, and he was going to do just that.

#9...MARGINAL ERROR

You know, sometimes reality imitates fiction.

Toby sat down at his desk and rested his elbows upon its flat surface. He flipped through one of his fantasy books before stuffing the socially-unacceptable reading material into the empty steel hollow beneath the flat wood he would be working over.

Seventh grade was hard, but even harder was not fitting in, and his mind was always on this unfortunate fact. He was a skinny nerd with glasses, though he distanced himself from that word, that terrible word "nerd," as much as he could.

He did not like the things the other kids in his grade liked. He did not like sports or crime shows or Boy Scouts or any of those things. He liked playing videogames and boardgames and tabletop roleplaying games with the few friends he did have...He did not like the things most people liked.

What he really wanted was a girlfriend. Every other boy in his class seemed to have one, but he didn't...He was lonely. He was an outcast. Nobody liked him.

Of course, it was a new decade, so maybe things would get better. It was October 1st of 1991, the Gulf War had ended months ago, and a new song on the radio—that one by Jesus Jones—inspired him every time he heard it, so he felt like things might actually be getting better after all.

It was something to hope for.

He was thinking about this as two girls sat down at their desks to his immediate left.

Those girls were Anna Bainbridge and Lorie Hartwick, but they never gave him the time of day. Nevertheless, they were gabbing away, and their conversation was just interesting enough to pull Toby out of his inner world of thought. It was a little difficult to hear them over everyone else in the room, everyone in here talking to each other at the same time, but Toby managed it anyway.

"They're not going to finish renovations before winter," said Lorie. "That's what I heard from my brother."

"The old part of the school was creepy anyway," replied Anna. "What are they even doing over there? Why do we even need renovations?"

"They have to take out something called 'asbestos,'" said Lorie. "But yeah, I wish they'd just tear it all down. The new building is so much better. At least, I think so."

She nodded once and leaned in toward Anna, and Toby had to strain to hear her.

"It's more than that, though," said Lorie in a hushed voice. "Didn't you hear about what happened to Rachel Gibbons?"

"She ran off last year," shrugged Anna. "I overheard my mom talking about it over the phone."

"No, she just disappeared," said Lorie with a shake of her head. "Vanished…and she was at school…in…the old…building."

"No way," said Anna as she rolled her eyes.

"Yes, way," nodded Lorie. "My older-brother's best-friend's cousin disappeared the year before that, back in '89. My brother told me someone goes missing every year."

"They run off," sighed Anna. "Don't be stupid. He's just saying that to scare you."

"Uh, uh," said Lorie. "Someone goes missing every year, and the police don't do anything about it. They just say the kids run off. I'm telling the truth."

"Oh, yeah?" asked Anna.

"Yeah," nodded Lorie. "My brother says it's a ghost. It lures you in and then kills you. You become a ghost after that. That's why the old building is haunted. Even the workers are afraid to work in there. They went on strike because of the ghost. That's why they're not working today."

"They're working on Friday, dummy," snorted Anna. "That's why we're getting Friday off. It's so they don't interrupt the school. Not to mention that if a ghost makes more ghosts, then there would be ghosts all over the place…Use some common sense. Your brother is pulling your leg."

"No, he isn't," said Lorie as she shook her head in adamant denial. "My brother hears everything from around town, like when they were going to fire that school janitor last year, Mr. Walsh, but they never got the chance to. They found kiddie porn in his office, but he disappeared before the police could pick him up. My brother says the parents around town secretly killed him."

"That's the plot to *A Nightmare on Elm Street*, doofus," frowned Anna. "Next, you're going to be telling me this guy came back in your dreams or something."

"No, but my aunt did have a nightmare like that," nodded Lorie. "She dreamed that Freddy Krueger was after her, and she woke up with slashes in her bedsheets."

"That is the dumbest thing I've ever heard!" laughed Anna. "Lorie, you are as gullible as a—"

Anna cut her sentence short, nudged Lorie, and both girls turned to glare at Toby. He had been engrossed in their conversation, so he had not realized he had been staring at them for the entirety of that conversation.

"Do you mind?" asked Anna, but her tone was not friendly.

Toby felt his cheeks burn a bright red as he moved his gaze forward. Class was going to start soon anyway.

"What a dork," he heard Lorie say.

Toby swallowed that insult and let it drown. He would try and forget about it, but he was going to have to push it down, deep down, for now. He did not like to be insulted, especially by girls, but class was going to start, so he had other things to worry about at the moment.

Mr. Redford, Toby's Social Studies teacher, walked in through the class door, but the man did not go to his desk like he normally would have. No, he walked straight up to Toby, but what the man wanted, Toby did not know.

The portly man with a pencil-thin mustache dropped one of Toby's fantasy books on Toby's desk.

"Here's your lost book, Tobe," said Mr. Redford matter-of-factly. "Someone dropped it off in the mail slot at the front office. Try not to lose it again."

Toby briefly looked through his books before realizing he did not have the book in question on him. He really must have dropped it at some point, but thankfully, someone had found it.

This particular book, "The Dragon's Secret Sword," was one Toby had already finished reading, but it still had Toby's red bookmark in it, Toby's specialty bookmark with his name on it, his name printed out in big, fancy, gold letters. He did not write his name in his books because he wanted them to remain pristine, in good condition, so it was a good thing that his named bookmark had been in the book, or he may have never seen his book again.

"All right!" said Mr. Redford. "Everybody, get out your Social Studies books and turn to page…"

Mr. Redford's voice trailed off as Toby focused the man out of his field of hearing. There was a far more pressing issue at hand.

Someone had written in his book.

Toby had flipped open the first page, and someone had written, "Hi! 37," in the upper right margin of page 1, that writing in flowery, bold, blue ink, that writing in *his* book, that writing a desecration to one of Toby's most-prized fantasy novels.

He saw the number "37" and the arrow next to it, and it occurred to him to turn to page 37, though why he thought this, he did not know. Perhaps it was curiosity, or perhaps it was anger, but he was going to check the rest of the book for damage anyway, so he flipped to page 37 without delay.

There was another note in the margin on page 37, this time in the lower right margin. It read, "I know you! 53."

Whoever had done this to his book wanted him to turn the pages, so he did. He was upset about the damage to his novel, but he also wanted to see what any other notes had to say, so he flipped to page 53.

The note in the margin on page 53 read, “I like you a lot! 72.”

Toby’s heart skipped a beat. He felt flushed and a little out of it…Was this what he had been waiting for? Was this his chance to be happy?

He quickly put his Social Studies book on his desk and flipped it open to a random page, pretending to be interested in class just like everyone else, but he had already ceased listening to Mr. Redford’s droning. No, he was engaged in this now.

Toby quietly flipped to page 72 as doubt ran through him. Maybe this girl didn’t know who he was. Maybe she had the wrong person…

The upper left margin on page 72 read, “Your mom picks you up after school, Toby. I know! 85.”

Toby nearly fainted after reading that. Not only did this girl like him, but she had been watching him…If only he knew who she was!

He turned to page 85, and the note in the margin read, “Let’s meet up after school! 89.”

Yes. Yes, he could do that. His mom was always fifteen minutes or more late. He could definitely meet up real fast…

He flipped the pages to page 89, and that note read, “We’ll meet here in school real fast! 107.”

This girl knew exactly what he was thinking, like she was…like she was his soulmate or something. Yes…that’s indeed what she was, his *soulmate*. He was going to meet his soulmate. He was going to meet someone who actually liked him for who he was, and she wasn’t mean; she was nice, not mean, not like Anna or Lorie.

Maybe she was an outcast like him. Maybe she was ugly or fat or…but…but…he didn’t care about that. No, his heart was pounding out of his chest, so he made his decision then and there to go meet her. He knew when to meet her, so now he just needed to know where.

He flipped to page 107. The note in the right margin read, “Don’t tell anyone. I’ll get made fun of…129.”

He had been wrong. She wasn’t ugly or fat. She was one of the popular girls, one of the pretty girls…She had to be. He was a nerd, a dork, but she was in love with him. She couldn’t be seen with him because he was a nerd…Yes, that was it; that’s what was going on.

Toby couldn’t breathe. This was incredible, his dream come true. Not only was he going to meet his soulmate, but she was one of the beautiful ones.

He was in heaven for a few brief seconds before the swift and commanding voice of Mr. Redford brought him back down to earth.

“Toby!” snapped the portly man. “Did you hear what I just said?”

Toby shoved his book into his desk and straightened up at attention. There would be time to flip through the pages later after class. He was certain the “where” he was looking for to meet up with his soulmate was further on in the book, but he would address that later. He knew better than to get in trouble now, so he would be patient for just a little while longer, as long as it took for the school day to end.

*****

Toby had his black backpack on his back, and all of his books were in it save one. No, the book he held in his hands, the book not tucked away in his backpack, was “The Dragon’s Secret Sword,” and he had it flipped open to page 129. The note in the margin on that page read, “Go past the gym! 136.”

He flipped to page 136 as he passed by the gym’s double doors. There were other kids at basketball practice in there right now, but he was not concerned with them. He needed the next instruction in order to find his one true love.

The note on page 136 read, “Sneak into the girls’ locker room! 149.”

His heart raced out of control. Meeting up with his soulmate was one thing, but sneaking into the girls’ locker room?...He didn’t have a lot of time before his mom arrived, and even then, someone at the front office might come looking for him, so he needed to man up and walk in there right now.

Hopefully, no naked girls were in there. It was every boy's dream to see a locker room full of naked girls, naked girls all wet from the shower, but Toby wasn't stupid. He didn't want to get arrested. Everyone would call him a pervert, and he'd probably be shipped off to a funny farm. He didn't want that.

A thought occurred to him, a dark one, a mean one. Maybe this was a prank. Maybe a bunch of girls had gotten together and were going to catch him in the girls' locker room, and…

No…No! He didn't believe that, and more importantly, he *wouldn't* believe that. This was real. He had a soulmate, his one true love, and he was going to find her. She was his princess in need of rescuing, and he was just the brave knight to quest after her.

"I am a brave knight," whispered Toby to himself.

He was going to go rescue his princess.

He slipped into the girls' locker room, feeling extremely dirty as he did, but…there was no one in the locker room or shower area anyway. She wasn't here, so maybe she was meeting him in here, or…

Toby turned the pages of his book until he hit page 149. The note in the margin of that page read, "Find the big locker nearest the showers! 158."

So that was it. There was probably a note or something in the…No, that couldn't be it. There was another page to turn to.

Toby found the big blue locker nearest the shower, a big blue locker that stood out amongst the royal-blue half-lockers that bedecked the small locker room. Of course, it was locked with a combination lock, but that meant…

He quickly flipped to page 158. The note in the margin read, "The combination is 04-07-28! 163."

He turned the combination lock with shaky hands. This was getting exciting!

He opened the locker door, and…

There was nothing in the locker. It was completely empty.

He flipped to page 163, and the margin note read, "Push hard on the back of the locker! 179."

Toby pushed on the back wall of the locker and immediately felt the metal push inwards, push free from whatever was holding it in place. It swung open on small interior hinges, and he could suddenly see into another locker, this one a grey locker with a closed grey locker door.

He turned to page 179 and read the note in that margin. It read, "Go in and shut the door behind you! Open the next door! 184."

He followed the instructions to the letter. He climbed into the locker, closed the door behind him, and opened the grey locker door before him.

He peered out into a dim hallway. There were lockers here and there, but there were also ladders along with plastic sheets draped around the area, tools like drills and hammers here and there, exposed wires in the roof tiles…

This was the old part of school. This was where they were doing renovations.

Toby turned to page 184. The note in the upper-lefthand margin read, "You're almost there! Go straight down the hall! 197."

The love in that flowery blue lettering spurred him onward. He was almost there, and his one true soulmate was waiting for him.

He turned to page 197 and read the note in that upper-right margin. It read, "I'll be in the girls' restroom! I'll be in the second stall! I'll be waiting for you!"

Toby practically flew down the hallway, jumping over tools, ducking under ladders, and running around hanging plastic tarps as he looked right and left for the first girls' restroom he could find.

After a few seconds of frantic searching, he saw a girls' restroom on his right, and he yanked open the heavy wooden door to it without a moment's hesitation.

The heavy door closed behind him as he walked into the lit restroom. The lights in this part of the school, the old part of the school, were shut off, all except for this restroom, but he was glad for that…At least he could see. He would be able to see with clear vision the girl of his dreams.

But it was time to throw all of his doubts aside and meet his one true love.

"Hello?" called out Toby. "I figured out your notes! I'm here to meet you!"

He walked up to the second stall door and gingerly opened it, breathless with anticipation, ready to see who this beautiful girl was, ready to start living for once…to hold his one true love in his arms…to kiss her sweet lips…

The door swung open as Toby stopped to stare at the figure before him.

In the stall was a big man, a big, big man in a grime-stained, janitor's, dark-blue uniform, that uniform with the white oval name tag of "Walsh" on it in curvy red letters, and over his fat face was a clear plastic Halloween mask with ruby lips and a red clown nose, speckled black eyelashes around the eyeholes, that mask a soulless epitome of extricated terror.

Toby's scream was cut short as a black plastic garbage bag wrapped its suffocating interior around his slender head.

#10...SHIMMER ON THE WATER

Ah, summer-camp hijinks.

Arnie picked up a stick and swung it in the air. He was at the very edge of the forest with his friends, right behind the cabins. Breakfast hadn't started yet, so they had a few minutes to goof off before going to the cafeteria.

He was there with his best friends at Camp Olenglade, because this was where the parents of the nearby town of Keywell sent their kids for the summer. It wasn't like Arnie or his friends wanted to be here, but it was better than doing nothing for the first nine weeks of their time away from school.

All of them wore the white T-shirts and forest-green shorts for the '76 campers at Olenglade, so Arnie felt like he was part of a team when he was with his friends, a united front against the world. Being united in something was important for thirteen-year-olds, even if that world was just summer camp.

"Have you seen that new Pepsi can?" asked Gordon.

Gordon was the biggest of them, stocky and broad-shouldered, the muscle of their team. Arnie likened him to their bully protection, their shield against getting picked on, but it wasn't like Arnie was a coward. He was their unofficial leader, after all. If there was ever any trouble, he and Gordon were first up and first in.

"Everybody's seen the new can," said Donnie. "It's the bicentennial."

Donnie was quick and scrappy, kind of a smart-mouth, but he was a good and loyal friend. Arnie could always count on him to come up with a quick retort.

"That's boring," said Arnie. "There's got to be something else to talk about while we've got a few minutes. I mean, we can talk at breakfast, but it's not the same. It's not just us there, you know?"

"No kidding," snorted Gordon. "We can't talk about anything we really like."

"Yeah," said Miles. "I can't talk about science fiction at all. I really wish they'd come out with a *Star Trek* movie."

Everyone else groaned.

"Not this again," frowned Donnie.

Miles was…well…the *different* one of their group. He wore glasses and was into reading science fiction and comic books. His interests were a little esoteric compared to everyone else. He mainly just tagged along with them, probably because no one else would take him.

"You're the only one who's ever watched that show, Miles," said Arnie as he rolled his eyes.

"*Watches*," corrected Miles. "I catch the reruns when I can."

"It's been what?" asked Gordon. "Like ten years since that show aired? Let it go. Watch something else…like *Kolchak*."

"Yeah, *The Night Stalker*," said Arnie. "I liked that series. Too bad it got canceled."

"They always cancel the good ones," said Donnie. "Remember *Night Gallery*?"

"Barely," said Arnie. "There's nothing ever playing on TV anymore."

"*Jaws* was awesome," said Gordon.

"Yeah, but you're the only one of us that's seen it," said Donnie. "Plus, you had nightmares for weeks last year. Serves you right for getting your mom and dad to take you on opening night."

"Shut up," frowned Gordon. "That movie is terrifying. You have no idea. No shark should be that big."

"Is scary stuff all you guys ever watch?" asked Miles.

"Pretty much," shrugged Arnie. "Heck, if investigating the supernatural was a real job, that's what I'd be doing when I grow up. I'd be investigating ghosts and witches and stuff like Kolchak."

"It's gotta beat selling cars," frowned Gordon. "That's what my dad does. He wants me to come help him out at the lot after camp is through, but I don't want to do that."

"My old man fixes cars," said Donnie. "He's a grease monkey."

"Yeah, yeah," nodded Arnie in facetious interest. "One sells 'em, one fixes 'em. Heard it a million times, guys. Miles' dad is a lawyer, and my dad is—"

"Hey!" called out an unfamiliar voice.

They all froze.

An older boy came walking up, this boy about fifteen or sixteen or so. He was tall, with short blond hair and blue eyes, and he wore a Camp Olenglade T-shirt, but his shirt was dark green like his shorts. Arnie had never seen him before.

Arnie was sure the others were thinking the same thing he was…Maybe they were all in trouble for something. Maybe they weren't supposed to be out here before breakfast.

"We're going to breakfast," said Arnie quickly. "We were just on our way."

"Eh, I don't care about that," said the older boy as he waved off Arnie. "No, I thought I heard something about scary stuff."

"Yeah?" asked Donnie. "What's it to ya?"

"I just wanted to know if you liked scary stuff," shrugged the new kid.

"Yeah," said Arnie carefully. "Who are you anyway?"

"Who are you?" asked the older boy.

"I'm Arnie," said Arnie. "This is Gordon, that's Donnie, and that's Miles."

"Well, I'm Casey," said the new boy. "I know everything about this camp…I even know about the Witch's Isle."

Now, this sounded interesting. Arnie had never heard of any "Witch's Isle." None of them had.

"Witch's Isle?" asked Gordon.

"Yeah," grinned this new boy, "Casey." "It's supposed to appear somewhere on the lake whenever there's a full moon."

"Full moons are for werewolves, not witches," scoffed Donnie.

"Oh, so you know your stuff, huh?" asked Casey. "Well, they say that the Isle is never in the same spot twice, and there's only one way to find it."

"Oh, yeah?" asked Donnie. "What's that?"

"You have to follow the spooklights," nodded Casey.

The older boy's blue eyes were wide as he nodded twice in eerie confirmation, a freaky grin on his face, but Arnie still had no idea what Casey was talking about. Arnie had never heard of any "Witch's Isle" or any "spooklights." In fact, he suspected this was just a prank anyway. Older boys liked to scare younger boys, especially at summer camp. It was an initiation thing.

"This sounds like a pretty weak ghost story," smirked Arnie. "We've heard 'em all. You'll have to do better than that."

"Yeah," said Donnie. "We watch horror for a living."

"Is that right?" asked Casey. "Well, what I'm talking about isn't a story…It's *real*."

"B.S.," said Gordon. "I've never heard of any 'Witch's Isle.' Have you guys ever heard of this?"

"Nope," said Arnie and Donnie at the same time.

They looked over to Miles, but their nerdy friend simply shrugged.

"It's there," nodded Casey. "It's there, and it's going to appear tonight out on the lake."

"Right," said Arnie as he rolled his eyes. "So, if it's there, how come no one I know has ever found it?"

"Because it's not common knowledge," said Casey.

"Then how do you know about it?" asked Donnie.

"I know everything about this camp," grinned the older boy. "I've been here every year since I was ten. That's how I know about Camp Olenglade's deepest, darkest secret."

"Yeah, yeah, mysterious isle, spooklights, whatever," said Donnie. "What's so scary about this 'Witch's Isle'?"

"The witch, of course," said Casey.

"And?" asked Arnie. "We've heard 'em all…uhhh…Casey. You can't scare us."

"Is that so?" asked the older boy. "Well, I bet you've never heard of Jenny Greenteeth."

"No," said Gordon flatly. "Are you gonna tell us about her?"

"Yeah," snorted Donnie. "Fill us in, smart guy."

"Jenny Greenteeth is an old swamp hag that preys on the elderly and the young," nodded Casey. "She has green skin like a toad, long green hair like swamp mush, black claws that rake and rend, and sharp green fangs."

"Hey, it's your girlfriend, Donnie," chuckled Gordon.

Arnie laughed right along with Miles at the impromptu dig, but Donnie was not appreciative of the joke.

"Yeah, yeah," said the wiry kid. "Eat a dead squirrel, Gordie."

"Anyway…" continued Casey. "Anyway, you can find Witch's Isle by following the spooklights that appear over the lake. Once you're on the Isle, you can follow the spooklights some more, and they'll lead you to Jenny."

They simply stared at the older boy as if he were full of it, which was what he was. There was no "Witch's Isle," "spooklights," or anything else like that.

"I'm going out on the lake tonight after lights out," said this new boy, "Casey." "If you guys wanna tag along, I could use more people than just me. I'm going to look for the spooklights to find Jenny."

"Right," sighed Arnie. "If this *were* real, somebody would have found this 'Jenny' by now…uhhh…Casey. We wouldn't be the first ones to do it…This is just a prank. This is a snipe hunt, or at best, looking for Bigfoot."

"Oh, so you *are* scared," grinned Casey. "I knew it."

"We're not scared," frowned Gordon. "This is just a prank anyway. We weren't born yesterday."

"Okay," shrugged the older boy. "I guess I'll go by myself, then. I'll just grab a camera, take pictures, and be a star. Why should I share the credit anyway?"

He turned to walk away, but Arnie thought better about his story.

"Wait," said Arnie. "Wait a second."

Casey turned around and gave Arnie a slight smirk.

"*Yeeeeees*?" asked the older boy.

"Are you just going by yourself?" asked Arnie.

"Yep," said Casey firmly.

"Eh, I guess I can go," shrugged Arnie. "There's nothing better to do here anyway…What do you guys think?"

"Yeah, whatever," said Donnie. "How 'bout it, Gordo?"

"Yeah, okay," said Gordon. "We don't have a camera, though."

"Miles has a camera," nodded Arnie.

They all turned to look at their least-associated "friend." Miles had a startled look on his four-eyed face, like a deer caught in the headlights.

"Don't be a chicken, Miles," sighed Arnie. "We're all going, and you're the only one with a camera. There aren't any spooklights or a Witch's Isle anyway. We're just taking a cruise out on the lake."

"But it's after hours, and—" started Miles.

"Oh, you baby," frowned Donnie. "Everybody screws around after hours. I saw Daryll Grouper and Millie Furley just last night. They were going out behind the cabins to fool around."

"Were you spying on the counselors again?" asked Gordon. "That's gross, Donnie."

"That's how you learn," shrugged Donnie.

"No thanks," frowned Gordon. "I walked in on my parents one time. Scarred me for life."

The older boy, Casey, laughed, and everyone else but Miles followed suit. Miles looked nervous and sweaty over the entire conversation, but Arnie just chalked that up to him being chicken.

"I don't know, guys," said Miles.

"Seriously, don't be a chicken, Miles," frowned Arnie. "If you wanna hang out with us, then you actually have to hang out with us…We need you anyway. You're the only one with a camera."

"I…guess," said Miles slowly, but Arnie could tell Miles wasn't convinced.

"Just show up at the docks tonight after lights out," said Casey with a timely intervention. "We'll all meet up at the docks tonight and take out the canoes…You boys know how to row?"

"Of course," snorted Donnie. "We already told you…We weren't born yesterday."

Arnie nodded and grinned. They were going to have themselves a little adventure, something to spice up camp life and something to talk about later on. It was going to be fun, the type of fun they rarely got to engage in…well…anywhere.

Arnie had been skeptical at first, but now he was looking forward to this nightly outing. In fact, it was a shame society didn't have summer camps dedicated to paranormal investigation.

But breakfast and the rest of the day awaited them. As much as it was a downer, they all still had to engage in "legitimate" camp activities. It's what their parents had paid for anyway.

*****

Arnie showed up at the docks with the others, lantern in hand. They all had their lanterns, though Miles had brought his camera as well.

Casey was not there yet, so they waited by the canoes, those canoes painted a bright red for visibility purposes.

"Guess he's not here yet," said Gordon.

"I told you this was a prank," said Donnie.

"We all thought it was a prank," pointed out Arnie. "Let's just give him a couple of minutes."

"I don't know about this, guys," said Miles.

They all groaned at Miles' reticence. He was really beginning to bug them.

"Don't chicken out now, Miles," frowned Arnie. "We're all here, and we're in this together."

"That's right," said Casey.

The older boy's voice ambushed them from behind.

Startled, Arnie turned and nearly dropped his lantern. Casey was standing on the dock with them, right by the canoes, but Arnie could have sworn he hadn't been there a second ago.

"Good grief, man!" barked Donnie. "Don't sneak up on us like that!"

"How did you even get around us?" asked Gordon in disbelief.

"I have my ways," grinned the older boy. "Now let's stop wasting time…Come on, ladies…Adventure awaits."

Gordon and Donnie took their lanterns and immediately boarded one of the canoes.

Arnie stepped into his own canoe and looked over toward Miles, but the four-eyed kid hesitated. He would not follow for some reason.

"Miles," frowned Arnie, "hop in."

"I…I don't want to do this," said Miles.

"Just get in the canoe," said Gordon. "Don't be a wuss."

"No," said Miles with a shake of his head. "I've got a bad feeling about this."

"Oh, come on!" sighed Arnie. "Just get in the boat!"

The boy shook his head no and set down his lantern. He pulled off his camera he was strap carrying and handed it to Arnie.

"Here," he said nervously. "You take the camera. I'm going back to the cabins."

"You wuss!" said Donnie.

"Something's not right about this," said Miles. "You guys can go. Just take pictures and show me."

"Come on, Miles," grinned Casey. "Join the fun. We're going to have fun."

Miles shook his head no again as he picked up his lantern.

"Something's not right," said the boy. "I've got a bad feeling…You…You guys shouldn't go, either. We should just go back."

"Pah," said Arnie as he waved him off. "You're no fun…Fine. We'll go and show you the pictures we take."

"I really don't think you guys should go," said Miles. "Something's bad here. I've got a bad feeling."

He stared directly at Casey, a stare that made Arnie pause for a second, but Casey simply grinned at Miles. It was like there was an unspoken message between the two boys, but what that message could be, Arnie had no idea.

"The only bad feelings you get is when you touch yourself at night," scoffed Donnie.

"Now, now," smiled Casey. "There's no reason to be crude, guys…Let him go. We'll be the ones to have fun. It's clear he doesn't want to have any."

Miles continued to stare at the older boy, but the four-eyed nerd shook in place, trembling, and Arnie couldn't help but wonder what had his friend so anxious.

"What's going on, Miles?" asked Arnie. "We're just going out on the water. It's not a big deal. It's not like there's a Witch's Isle anyway."

"You shouldn't go," said Miles. "I don't think you should go."

He continued to stare at Casey, but this was a little unnerving, even for someone as steadfast as Arnie.

"Let's just go, boys," grinned Casey. "Miles can go on back."

"*Yeeeeeah,*" drawled out Arnie.

He was sensing something was off here, as if Miles knew or understood something he did not.

But Arnie was still going. He was not going to miss out on this. It was way too much fun.

"You just go on back, Miles," said Arnie. "We'll catch you when we come back and fill you in. I'll get your camera back to you."

He turned his attention back upon their older chaperone.

"It looks like you don't have to take your own boat, Casey," said Arnie. "You can come with me."

There was nothing more to say after that. Arnie put the strap of the camera around his right shoulder, and there was a certain finality to that action that no one else could argue with.

The older boy, Casey, entered Arnie's canoe, and they all pushed off from the dock without another spoken word.

They rowed out onto the lake, but Arnie took a moment to look behind himself, and there was Miles, still standing on the dock, lantern in hand, staring at them all, watching them leave. That chicken was acting as if he'd never see any of them again…It really was unsettling.

"I wonder what's gotten into him?" asked Arnie quietly. "It's like he's spooked or something."

"He's just a wet blanket," said Casey. "Ignore him."

They rowed for a bit, the two canoes in close proximity to each other, and then Casey nodded toward the distance, out toward the middle of the lake.

"Speaking of spooked, look out there," he said in a hushed voice.

Arnie squinted as he tried to peer through the darkness. They had their lanterns in their boats, and that was good, and the light of the full moon was out, and that was also good, but it was still difficult to see.

There was a shimmer on the water at first, and then an orb of golden light appeared over that water, rising up from the depths, a crackling of lightning in a ball that could not be heard but could definitely be seen. It was big, bigger than a basketball, and Arnie could tell that size even from the distance they were at.

"Holy crap!" he barked out. "Are you guys seeing this!"

"Of course, we're seeing it!" barked back Donnie. "What are you waiting for! Take a picture of it, dingus!"

"Yeah, yeah," said Arnie.

He took off the lens cap, adjusted the flash meter, and raised the camera viewport up to his right eye. It was a good thing he knew how to use a camera, or he'd have probably left the lens cap on or the flash off.

He snapped a couple of pictures of the ball of light in the distance.

"That's a spooklight," said Casey. "We need to follow it to find the Isle."

"There may be a spooklight," argued Gordon, "but that doesn't mean there's any Witch's Isle."

"Then let's find out if there is one," said Casey.

They rowed closer to the orb in the distance, but Arnie thought better about something, something he had missed before.

"I thought you said you were bringing a camera, too," he said.

"I did," said Casey.

The older boy produced a camera in his right hand, one that was very similar to Miles' camera, right down to the same type of strap. In fact, Casey had the thing strapped around his shoulder, but Arnie could have sworn he had not seen any such thing before just now.

"Where did you get that?" asked Arnie.

"I've had it the whole time," said the older boy. "You're not very observant, are you?"

Arnie shook his head at that. His memory was playing tricks on him.

The older boy took a moment to take a couple of pictures of the glowing orb in the distance.

"Let's go after it," he said after lowering his camera.

The four boys grabbed the oars of their canoes, and they were off after that, off toward following the mysterious orb of crackling light hovering over the still waters of the lake.

It was not long before the orb began to move, but they were only halfway to it.

"Row, Donnie!" huffed Gordon.

"I am!" huffed back the wiry boy.

Arnie did not waste any breath giving any kind of comment or order. No, he rowed as hard as he could, keeping up with Casey's rowing as best he could.

"We've got to…got to catch it," huffed Gordon.

They rowed for the ball of light in the distance, but it continued to move across the lake, always just out of reach. Nevertheless, none of them were about to give up now.

"There it goes!" huffed Arnie. "It's turning right!"

They all struggled to turn their canoes as the ball of crackling energy made a swift turn right, hovering for a second as if waiting for them, and then it took off again toward the east side of the lake.

"It's like it's got a mind of its…of its own!" huffed Donnie.

"Just row!" huffed Gordon.

"I am!" barked Donnie.

"Push it, guys!" ordered Casey. "We have to follow it!"

Arnie rowed and rowed until it felt like his arms were going to fall off.

The ball of light moved into a stationary position. Its electric, golden glow lit up the gnarled trunk and arms of an old, leafless, withered tree, but there was only one problem with this…They were all still in the middle of the lake.

"What the hell!" huffed Gordon.

"I see it!" barked Arnie.

The older boy, Casey, turned and shone Arnie a wide grin.

"There it is," said Casey. "The Witch's Isle."

"This is insane," puffed out Arnie.

They rowed until they could clearly see the edges of the tiny isle out in the middle of the lake.

"Let's get closer and get some pictures," said Arnie.

They rowed up to the edge of solid land.

They were now closer than they'd ever been to the glowing orb, its large shape crackling and streaming light without any sound, right next to the dead tree in the center of this isle, that tree a mere thirty feet away.

"There it is," whispered Donnie.

"Everybody, out," ordered Casey.

Arnie stepped out onto dry land without thinking twice. The others exited the canoes, and all four of them dragged the canoes far enough onto the mild shoreline so that the boats did not wander off.

Arnie took his lantern from the boat as the others removed theirs. They were going to need some light source other than the moon and whatever that weird orb was.

They all stared at the ball of light hovering next to the old withered tree, and they stared at it for a full thirty seconds before any of them said a word. It was Donnie who broke that silence, because the wiry kid could never keep his mouth shut for long.

"Is this real?" asked Donnie.

"I don't know," said Arnie. "If it's a trick, it's a really elaborate one."

"Well, what are we waiting for?" asked Gordon. "You've got Miles' camera, Arnie, and Casey has his own camera, so let's go check this thing out."

"Yeah," agreed Arnie.

They took a few steps toward the tree in the distance before their outdoorsman shoes sank into thick muck. Arnie pulled back his foot and looked down at the film of green algae that had formed over what had to be thick water and mud.

"Ugh…" he said unhappily. "This is some kind of marsh or bog or something."

"No pain, no gain," grinned Donnie as he waded right in.

The boy waded waist deep into the greenish water without batting an eye. He made it about five feet before he turned and gave everyone else an irritated look.

"Well, are you coming or not?" asked Donnie.

"Yeah, all right," said Gordon.

The big kid waded in after Donnie, so Arnie waded in after them both.

He could feel the cold of the water sink into him.

"Whew!" he said as he shivered. "This is bracing!"

"No kidding," said Gordon. "Let's hurry and check this thing out. I wonder if we can touch it?"

"I don't know," said Donnie. "We should be careful about that."

"Yeah," said Arnie. "Baby steps, guys."

He held up his lantern in his left hand and Miles' camera in his right. It was going to be tricky taking a picture this way, but he'd figure something out. He'd just get Donnie to hit the snap button, now that he was thinking about it.

They waded out close to the tree, but the going was somewhat slow.

Donnie came within five feet of the orb, but he stopped as he gazed upon it.

Gordon came up beside him and looked over the bright ball of crackling luminescence.

"There's no sound or heat or anything coming from it," said Donnie quietly. "It just feels…cold."

"Yeah," said Gordon just as quietly.

Arnie sidled in next to Donnie, and he could feel the drop in temperature the moment he had come within that fateful five feet. There was definitely a pulse or aura of cold air coming off of this thing, as if he were standing directly in front of an air conditioner or an open refrigerator.

"What is this thing?" he asked in a hushed voice.

"Take a picture of it," said Gordon.

"Donnie, you'll have to hit the snap button once I have the picture lined up," said Arnie.

"Right," said Donnie.

Arnie was about to raise Miles' camera to his right eye when he was interrupted by the sound of Casey's distant voice.

"Oh, boys!" yelled the older kid. "You forgot something!"

They turned around, and there was Casey, still on the shore near the canoes, his lantern held high, his face etched with a weird grin.

"What!" yelled back Gordon.

The older boy replied to Gordon's query, but his voice took on a quiet, sinister tone. As quiet as that sinister reply had been, Arnie could still make out what Casey was saying, and he did not like the implications of it one bit.

"You forgot about Jenny," grinned the older boy.

Arnie turned and looked toward the orb he had been about to photograph. The large ball of crackling, golden luminescence sank down into the mud right next to the old withered tree, and then it was gone, vanishing without a trace.

"What in the—" began Donnie.

The wiry kid made a jerking motion, dropping his lantern into the marsh. He disappeared beneath the green-slicked water after that, only to pop up gasping for air a second later.

"Donnie, what the hell!" cursed Gordon.

"Something bit me!" yelped Donnie.

"Stop screwing around," said Gordon angrily. "You dropped your lantern, and now we have to find it!"

"No!" screeched Donnie. "Something bit me! There's something in the water!"

"You're only doing this because I watched *Jaws*," frowned Gordon. "Cut it out, you—"

Donnie did not reply, at least, not in the way Gordon had wanted. The wiry kid disappeared under the water again, vanishing into that green-slicked muck, and then he popped back up, splashing and sputtering, gasping for air. The boy screamed a second later, his body was thrashed about left and then right and then left and then right again, and then he vanished altogether as he was pulled beneath the thick green water.

"Donnie!" yelled Gordon.

Arnie's adrenaline spiked to the moon. His fight or flight kicked in, and he reacted without thinking.

"Run!" he yelled, but wading through thick marsh was the best he could do.

He turned and willed his muscles to move his body through the mire.

"Donnie!" yelled Gordon again.

Arnie briefly turned and realized the big kid was still looking for their friend.

Gordon held his lantern high in his right hand, his chubby face a mask of shock and fear.

"Run, Gordie!" yelled Arnie. "He's gone! Donnie's gone!"

The black and green water in front of Gordon erupted in an explosion as something burst from the bog and then splashed back down into it. For a mere half-a-second, Arnie wondered if Donnie had reappeared, but that wondering vanished in a puff of stage smoke as Gordon lazily turned around in a half spin.

The right side of the big kid's face was raked open, a rending of red lines and torn flesh, his right eye dangling slightly out of the right socket, and then he fell forward, pitching into the muck to splash and sink into the green bog.

Arnie waded back toward the shore without another word, wading back toward the watching form of Casey, the older boy simply standing there, lantern in hand, that weird grin still plastered across his handsome face.

"Help me!" yelled Arnie.

No sound came from Casey as the older boy morphed from his shoes up, glowing and changing simultaneously, and then there was nothing but a large and crackling golden orb where he had once stood.

Arnie could hear a faint laughter as the golden orb ten feet away from him moved back out onto the lake, leaving behind a faint shimmer on the water.

Arnie briefly turned to look back toward where his friends had sunk into this miniature marsh, but as he spun around, his lantern light revealed the green and brown face of the old hag, that terrifying face surrounded by a mop of marsh-muck hair, her grin a wide row of sharp, moss-green fangs glistening with the sanguine crimson of fresh blood, her skin bumpy and green like the armored leather of an alligator, her spindly and knotted fingers bedecked with long, razor-sharp, blackened nails.

There was a shimmer on the still and black waters of the lake. A loud and pitched, piercing scream echoed across the night, and then a silence descended, not so much as the croak of a frog or the buzz of a mosquito to fill that void.

*****

The two counselors, Daryll and Millie, had Miles sit down in a wooden office chair. Daryll sat down behind the office desk in his own chair, and Millie planted her butt on the edge of that desk. Both counselors gave Miles the staredown, but Miles could not stand their damning gazes for long.

"Where are they, Miles?" asked Daryll.

"We know you know," said Millie. "Did they go out on the lake last night? There were two canoes floating out—"

"Yes!" broke Miles.

It was, unfortunately, easy for him to break. He simply couldn't stand the pressure…He knew he'd never make it in prison.

The two counselors stared at each other for a second before staring back at Miles…He really couldn't withstand those damning gazes.

"I think you'd better tell us everything," said Daryll.

Miles began to spill his guts in rapid speech, a vocal typing out of verbality by his mouth moving upon its own accord.

"We were all talking yesterday morning," he rattled off, "and then this new kid walked up, and he was fifteen or sixteen, a couple years older than us, and he talked about some mysterious isle that appears on the lake every full moon, and he said his name was Casey, and he just appeared out of nowhere on the docks, and I saw him just appear out of thin air—"

"Whoa, wait, what?" asked Daryll. "Slow down, Miles. Take a deep breath. You're going too fast."

"Wait…Did you say Casey?" asked Millie. "As in Casey Olen?"

Miles shrugged. That boy had never mentioned his last name.

"He said his name was Casey," he repeated. "That's all I know. There was something creepy about him. I got a bad vibe from him."

The two counselors looked at each other for a moment, and then Daryll shook his head and rolled his eyes.

"Is that old ghost story still going around?" he asked.

Miles felt his heart stop for a brief second.

"Ghost…story?" he asked slowly.

"The ghost of Casey Olen has been going around since the '50s," said Millie. "They were still telling that one back when I was your age. I honestly thought it was dead by now…Guess not."

"Wha…What ghost story?" stammered Miles.

"There's no one at camp named Casey," said Daryll firmly. "That's one of the other kids pulling your leg. The camp-founders' son, Casey, disappeared back in 1952. He'd gone off looking for some vanishing island that supposedly had a witch on it. Everybody was convinced he'd run off, but there's been a persistent story that he found his island and the witch got him."

"And now he haunts the camp grounds," nodded Millie. "The whole thing is really stupid. It's just a campfire tale."

Miles felt his blood pressure drop as he paled from this revelation.

"Hey, are you okay?" asked Daryll. "Miles?…Hello?...You look pretty pale, buddy."

Miles was in a daze over all of this, but his mouth still spoke without his own volition.

"I knew he'd just appeared out of nowhere," he said slowly. "I knew it. I saw him appear out of nowhere…He just popped into existence…I saw it…I saw it, and I told them not to go, but I didn't…I didn't stop them…"

His breathing quickened to the point where he could no longer breathe, a counterintuitive process in his own mind, and then Miles' vision went black as he fainted dead away.

*****

Abbie kicked up a pile of leaves and sighed. She was at the very edge of the forest with her friends, right behind the cabins. They had a few minutes before breakfast started, and this was wasting time, but it wasn't like there was anything to do here anyway.

"This is *soooooo* boring!" she groaned.

She'd made some new friends here at Camp Olenglade, but even they couldn't stave off the sheer drollness and "ugh" of this place. It wasn't like any of them wanted to be here, but this was one of the few real summer camps left in the state, so this was a natural place to ship off a kid when parents wanted the summer to themselves.

All of them wore the light-green T-shirts and forest-green shorts for the '22 campers at Olenglade, so Abbie felt like she was part of a team when she was with her friends, a united front against the world. Being united in something was important for thirteen-year-olds, even if that world was just a godawful summer camp.

"Did they have to confiscate our phones?" asked Angela.

Angela was the pretty girl, tall and slender and blonde, the representative of their team. Abbie likened her to their get-out-of-jail-free card, their shield against getting in trouble, but it wasn't like Abbie was ugly. She was their unofficial leader, after all. If there was ever any trouble, she and Angela were first up and first in.

"It's because of that whole, stupid, camp-experience thing," said Madison as she rolled her eyes. "We're supposed to be roughing it."

Madison was the quick-witted one of their group, kind of a foul-mouth, but she was a good and loyal friend. Abbie could always count on her to come up with a quick and dirty insult.

"That's boring," said Abbie. "This whole camp is like being in a coma. There's nothing to do here, and what makes it worse is that our parents actually shelled out money for this. Now I feel like I can't waste the big bucks they paid for these nine weeks of babysitting."

"Yeah," sighed Gina. "I really wanted to binge *Gilmore Girls* again over the summer. I was going to do a marathon, starting with the pilot."

Everyone else groaned.

"Not this again," frowned Madison.

Gina was...well...the *different* one of their group. She wore glasses and was into reading romance books and manga. Her interests were a little esoteric compared to everyone else. She mainly just tagged along with them, probably because no one else would take her.

"You're the only one who's ever watched that show, Gina," said Abbie as she rolled her eyes.

"*Watches*," corrected Gina. "I like to watch it when I can."

"It's been what?" asked Angela. "Like over twenty years since that show aired? Let it go. Watch something else...like *Stranger Things*."

"Yeah, *Stranger Things*," said Abbie. "I like that series. Can't wait for the next season."

"It'll probably get canceled," said Madison. "They always cancel the good ones. Remember *Grimm*?"

"Barely," said Abbie. "There's nothing ever streaming anymore."

"*Freaks* was awesome," said Angela.

"Yeah, but you're the only one of us that's seen it," said Madison. "Even though it was made in the 1930s, my parents won't let me watch it...Ugh. The rest of us don't have access to the better stuff. Plus, you had nightmares about it. Serves you right for getting your mom and dad to let you watch it."

"Shut up," frowned Angela. "That movie is terrifying. You have no idea. No woman should ever end up like that."

"Is scary stuff all you guys ever watch?" asked Gina.

"Pretty much," shrugged Abbie. "Heck, if battling the supernatural was a real job, that's what I'd be doing when I'm an adult. I'd be fighting ghosts and demons and stuff like Sam and Dean from *Supernatural*."

"It has to be better than working at a big company," frowned Angela. "That's what my mom does. I'd rather be an influencer than do that."

"My mom's in retail," said Madison. "My dad makes all the money. He's an IT technician."

"Yeah, yeah," nodded Abbie in facetious interest. "Everyone's a corporate zombie. Heard it a million times, guys. Gina's mom is a lawyer, and my dad is—"

"Hey!" called out an unfamiliar voice.

They all froze.

An older boy came walking up, this boy about fifteen or sixteen or so. He was tall, with short blond hair and blue eyes, and he wore a Camp Olenglade T-shirt, but his shirt was dark green like his shorts. He was very cute in the face, a real hottie, but Abbie had never seen him before.

Abbie was sure the others were thinking the same thing she was…Maybe they were all in trouble for something. Maybe they weren't supposed to be out here before breakfast.

"We're going to breakfast," said Abbie quickly. "We were just on our way."

"Eh, I don't care about that," said the older boy as he waved her off. "No, I thought I heard something about scary stuff."

"Yeah?" asked Madison. "And?"

"I just wanted to know if you liked scary stuff," shrugged the older boy.

"Yeah," said Abbie carefully. "Yeah, we do…Who are you anyway?"

"Who are you?" asked the older boy.

"I'm Abbie," said Abbie. "This is Angela, that's Madison, and that's Gina."

"Well, I'm Casey," said the new boy. "I know everything about this camp…I even know about the Witch's Isle."

Now, this sounded interesting. Abbie had never heard of any "Witch's Isle." None of them had.

"Witch's Isle?" asked Angela.

"Yeah," grinned this new boy, "Casey." "It's supposed to appear somewhere on the lake whenever there's a full moon."

"Full moons are for werewolves, not witches," scoffed Madison.

"Oh, so you know your stuff, huh?" asked Casey. "Well, they say that the Isle is never in the same spot twice, and there's only one way to find it."

"Oh, yeah?" asked Madison. "And what's that?"

"You have to follow the spooklights," nodded Casey.

The older boy's blue eyes were wide as he nodded twice in eerie confirmation, a freaky grin on his face, but Abbie still had no idea what Casey was talking about. She had never heard of any "Witch's Isle" or any "spooklights." In fact, she suspected this was just a prank anyway. Boys liked to scare girls, especially at summer camp. It was a flirtation thing.

"This sounds like a pretty weak ghost story," smirked Abbie. "We've heard 'em all. You'll have to do better than that."

"Yeah," said Madison. "We watch horror for a living."

"Is that right?" asked Casey. "Well, what I'm talking about isn't a story…It's *real.*"

"Nonsense," said Angela. "I've never heard of any 'Witch's Isle.' Have you guys ever heard of this?"

"Nope," said Abbie and Madison at the same time.

They looked over to Gina, but their nerdy friend simply shrugged.

"It's there," nodded Casey. "It's there, and it's going to appear tonight out on the lake."

"Right," said Abbie as she rolled her eyes. "So, if it's there, how come no one I know has ever found it?"

"Because it's not common knowledge," said Casey.

"Then how do you know about it?" asked Madison.

"I know everything about this camp," grinned the older boy. "I've been here every year since I was ten. That's how I know about Camp Olenglade's deepest, darkest secret."

"Yeah, yeah, mysterious isle, spooklights, whatever," said Madison. "What's so scary about this 'Witch's Isle'?"

"The witch, of course," said Casey.

"And?" asked Abbie. "We've heard 'em all…uhhh…Casey. You can't scare us."

"Is that so?" asked the older boy. "Well, I bet you've never heard of Jenny Greenteeth."

"No," said Angela flatly. "And?...Continue, please."

"Yeah," snorted Madison. "Tell us about this 'Jenny.'"

"Jenny Greenteeth is an old swamp hag that preys on the elderly and the young," nodded Casey. "She has green skin like a toad, long green hair like swamp mush, black claws that rake and rend, and sharp green fangs."

"Hey, it's your girlfriend, Maddie," chuckled Angela.

Abbie laughed right along with Gina at the impromptu dig, but Madison was not appreciative of the joke.

"Yeah, yeah," said the foul-mouthed girl. "Go choke on your mom's fat—."

"Anyway…" continued Casey. "Anyway, you can find Witch's Isle by following the spooklights that appear over the lake. Once you're on the Isle, you can follow the spooklights some more, and they'll lead you to Jenny."

They simply stared at the older boy as if he were full of it, which was what he was. There was no "Witch's Isle," "spooklights," or anything else like that.

"I'm going out on the lake tonight after lights out," said this new boy, "Casey." "If you ladies wanna tag along, my friends and I could always use more people. We're going to look for the spooklights to find Jenny."

This boy was out of Abbie's league, but not out of Angela's. It would be awkward if they all went out witch chasing with him, because her friends were seriously competitive when it came to a hottie like Casey, and she already knew Angela would win him over pretty quickly anyway, but…

"Wait a minute, Casey…Did you say friends?" asked Abbie.

They heard the crunching of outdoorsman shoes on leaves and twigs. They all turned to view three new boys walking up to them, though these boys were the same age as they were, not older, not like Casey.

An athletic redheaded boy with a cute face walked up to Abbie and smiled.

"Hi," he said in a friendly tone. "I'm Arnie."

Abbie smiled inside. This boy was cute and definitely not out of her league. It occurred to her that Angela could have Casey, and Madison and Gina could fight over the other two.

This was like a perfect match for them all out of nowhere. In fact, this summer-camp hell was turning out to be fun after all.

“Witch chasing with you guys?” asked Abbie. “Sounds like fun! Count me in!”

About the Author

Mr. Marlott has a background in psychology and classic literature, and he enjoys literature of all types and genres. Mr. Marlott lives somewhere within the United States, has two Gen-Z children, and enjoys telling stories to anyone who will listen.

Books and Sites

You can read new stories of mine for free at bloodytwine.com. This site is my workshop where I work on new stories and perfect them for publication.

For more twisted tales with twisted endings, you can purchase *Bloody Twine #1-5* wherever they are sold.

If you want the basic building blocks to writing genre fiction, you can explore my two cents on the subject in *The Quick and Easy Guide to Writing Genre Fiction*.

For great cosmic horror, you can read some awesome eldritch-horror tales by Bert S. Lechner. You can purchase Mr. Lechner's collection of cosmic horror, *The Roots Grow into the Earth*, wherever it is sold. You can also check out Mr. Lechner's personal website at bertwriteshorror.com.

For a mix of traditional horror and cosmic horror, check out some incredible short stories by James Dermond. You can purchase Mr. Dermond's Doorways to the Unseen series wherever it is sold. You can also visit Mr. Dermond's website at jamesdermond.com.

If you like this book, give it a good review and tell me what your favorite story was in this bundle.

THE BLOODY TWINE SERIES

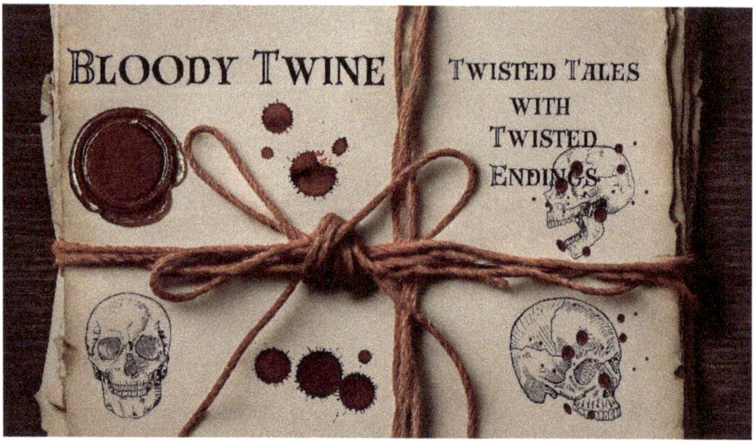

Welcome to the Bloody Twine Series, a collection of short horror stories written specifically for horror fans everywhere. These books contain a minimum of 10 traditional short horror stories for the collections, a minimum of 5 traditional short horror stories for the selections, and one traditional short horror novelette or novella for the presentations, all for your terrifying entertainment, so go someplace quiet, dim the lights, sit back, and enjoy some twisted tales with twisted endings.

Imagine walking into an abandoned storage room filled with old newspapers and magazines, all articles stacked in bundles neatly tied with twine, but then you discover other bundles, bundles not so neatly tied, ragged bundles of yellowed and partially-charred paper tied in bloodstained twine.

You see, some stories are meant to educate, and some stories are meant to entertain, but some stories…some stories are simply looking for a victim.

Enjoy.

Matthew L. Marlott

THE QUICK AND EASY GUIDE TO WRITING GENRE FICTION

Thinking of writing your own tale of love, redemption, and heroics? Writing genre fiction is an art, and *The Quick and Easy Guide to Writing Genre Fiction* provides the building blocks for being successful in this art. Learn all of the necessary techniques to get yourself started with writing in your chosen genre. Whether you're writing a mystery, a romance, a thriller, science-fiction, horror, fantasy, or any other genre, you'll have the foundation for writing great stories right here at your fingertips in this guide.

Included in this guide is a step-by-step instruction of what it takes to put together your creation in any genre. Also included in this guide is the complete creation process of an original short story by author Matthew L. Marlott, so you, too, can have an easy example of how to create your own stories, whether those stories are short stories, novels, or novellas. You'll be able to create your own worlds and your own universes, so learn the basics of writing genre fiction for the purpose of selling, for publication on a site, for fanfiction, or just for your own personal satisfaction.

Remember, if you want real life, you can just walk out the front door. Why not write down your own story on paper or screen instead? Get started with your journey into genre fiction by learning from this invaluable guide. Don't wait until you're on your deathbed. Get started today.

Matthew L. Marlott

THE ROOTS GROW INTO THE EARTH

"In the dark we found them…"

The Roots grow into the Earth. Unseen conduits of Power, growing through the darkness of the void; walkways for malevolent, eldritch things to travel, connecting their dead worlds to ours.

In this collection of nine short stories and novelettes, you will find tales of unfathomable predators, cosmic gods, dark magic, and the people who cross their path: from archaeologists, long on the search for the find of the century, ensnared by a being beyond their understanding, to a man who notices a detail on a wall in his house for the first time, unwittingly inviting the attention of a malefic force from beyond the stars.

The Roots Grow Into the Earth consists of nine of Bert S. Lechner's previously published works, including three stories available as standalone eBooks: Interstate, the Wall, and Joanne's Vault.

Bert S. Lechner

DOORWAYS TO THE UNSEEN

"The Doorways to the Unseen series is a collection of short story books from author James Dermond. The stories take the reader around the world and through time, with each tale offering a glimpse into a supernatural episode. Every volume in the series contains six short horror stories meant to chill the blood and inspire unimaginable terror in their readers.

"So, step inside and find that which has been hidden from you all along. Where the unknown and the unimaginable meet."

James Dermond

Until Next Time...

Bloody Twine #4

Twisted Tales with Twisted Endings